An Odyssey Home

A Winnipeg Novella

Carol McCullough

1027

Press

An Odyssey Home: A Winnipeg Novella
Copyright © 2024 by Carol McCullough

This is a work of fiction. For historical purposes, some political figures, street names, schools, and buildings are identified. However, all addresses of family homes, names, characters, and events in this book are either the product of the author's imagination or used in a fictitious manner. Any resemblance to actual persons, living or dead, or actual events is purely coincidental.

Editor: Leslie Malkin
Map Design: Ryan East and Carol McCullough
Cover Image: praire-towns.com
Contact Information: 1027Press@gmail.com

ISBN: 978-1-7382418-0-4

First Edition: November 2024

1027 Press

To my parents: thank you for choosing Winnipeg as our home.

AND

To all Winnipeggers: those living now, those who lived before and those who are yet to be.

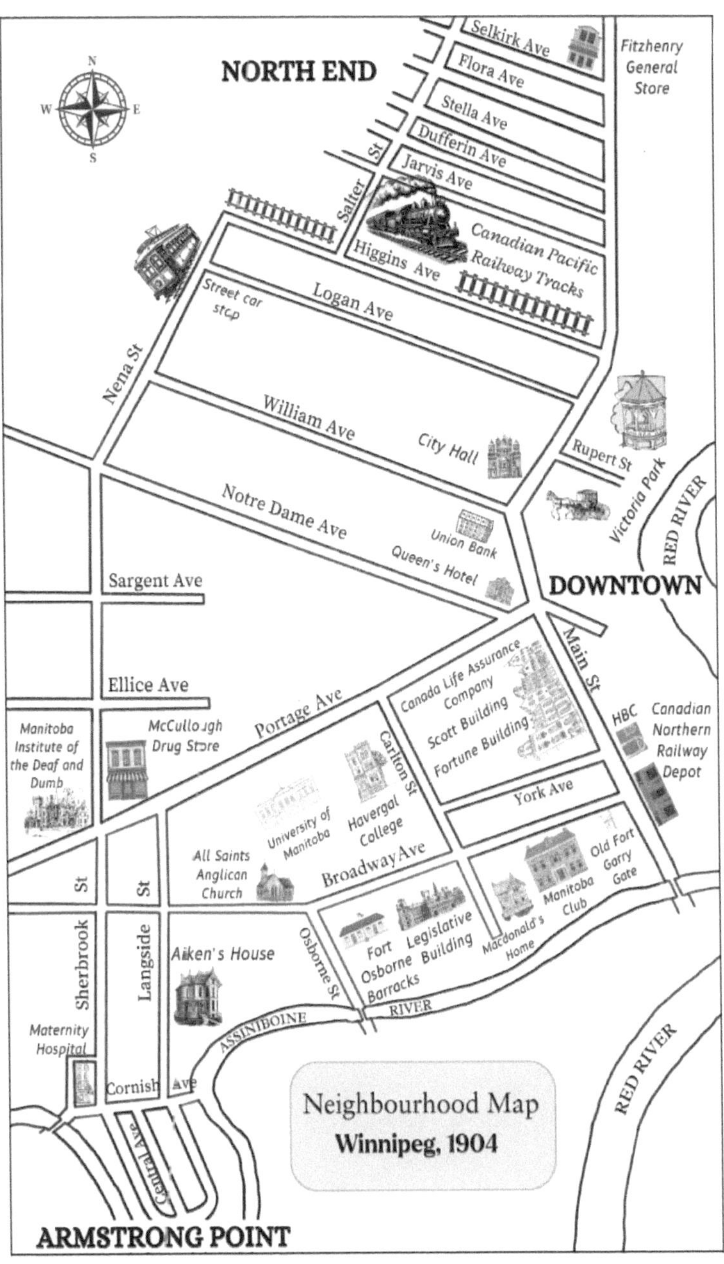

NORTH END
N
W E
S
Selkirk Ave
Flora Ave
Stella Ave
Dufferin Ave
Jarvis Ave
Salter St
Fitzhenry General Store
Canadian Pacific Railway Tracks
Higgins Ave
Street car stop
Logan Ave
Nena St
William Ave
City Hall
Rupert St
Victoria Park
RED RIVER
Notre Dame Ave
Union Bank
Queen's Hotel
DOWNTOWN
Sargent Ave
Ellice Ave
Main St
Portage Ave
Canada Life Assurance Company
Scott Building
Fortune Building
HBC
Canadian Northern Railway Depot
Manitoba Institute of the Deaf and Dumb
McCullough Drug Store
Carlton St
University of Manitoba
Havergal College
York Ave
All Saints Anglican Church
Broadway Ave
Macdonald's Home
Manitoba Club
Old Fort Garry Gate
Sherbrook St
Langside St
Aiken's House
Osborne St
Fort Osborne Barracks
Legislative Building
Maternity Hospital
Cornish Ave
Central Ave
ASSINIBOINE RIVER
RED RIVER
Neighbourhood Map
Winnipeg, 1904
ARMSTRONG POINT

CHAPTER 1

Monday, September 23, 2024

Graveyards are fascinating. All the lives lived. All the stories that could be told. What had happened to them? These were some of the thoughts going through seventeen-year-old Margaret's head as she walked around the St. James Cemetery. From her research on the cemetery, she knew the first burial had taken place in 1856 and there were now more than 9000 people buried in the cemetery. Margaret had been hoping to find some inspiration for her history essay which was due in two days. She was to write 1000 words about a Canadian. As Winnipeg was celebrating its 150th year as a city, Margaret had thought she would write about an historical Winnipegger. The cemetery was certainly a who's-who of Winnipeg: Chapman, Fiddler, McDermot, Bannatyne and Inkster. Those people all had streets or schools in Winnipeg named after them. But there were so many other names: Phillips, Hislop, Cooper, Mills and Patterson. Who were they?

Margaret glanced at her phone. It was five o'clock. She had come to the cemetery after school and had only meant to walk around for half an hour but now she realized she had been there for almost two hours. Her grandmother was coming over for dinner and her parents would be expecting her home soon.

It was a short drive back to her house on Middle Gate, in Armstrong Point, and Margaret took the time to reflect on how much history could be found in a cemetery and how she wanted to tell some of that history in her essay. When she walked into her house, her mom and grandmother were in the kitchen.

"Hi, Mom. Hi, Nana. Sorry I'm late. I was doing some research for my history paper and sort of lost track of time."

"No problem," said Nana. "I just got here. What type of research were you doing?"

"I was at the St. James Cemetery. You know, the one across from Polo Park?" Both her mom and Nana nodded.

"I thought I might find a name of someone buried there that I could do my paper on. I don't mean a famous person like a politician or a businessman. I was thinking of a regular person. Maybe a woman who contributed to the city."

"Well, I think Mrs. Sharpe would find that an excellent choice for an essay," said her mom.

Margaret and Nana exchanged smiles. Margaret attended the same school her mom had gone to, and Mrs. Sharpe had been one of her mom's teachers, too. Nana had also been a teacher at the school while her mom was a student there, so Nana and Mrs. Sharpe had been colleagues. It's a small world, but that's Winnipeg. Even with a population of more than 830,000 people, everyone seemed to know everyone.

"Hey there," said Margaret's dad as he came into the kitchen. "How was your day?"

"Good. School was busy and then after school I started thinking about my history essay. Maybe we can talk about it at dinner," said Margaret.

Over dinner, Margaret asked about some of the history of Armstrong Point. She learned their house had been built in 1913 and by then, there were several homes in the area. Some of the first homes had been built in the late 1880s. The conversation got Margaret thinking more about her essay and after dinner, she decided to start working on it.

Upstairs in her room, Margaret began to research Winnipeg and Armstrong Point. After becoming a city in 1874, Winnipeg's population had grown rapidly from its first 2000 inhabitants. There had been 26,000 people in 1891, 42,000 in 1901, 90,000 in 1906 and 150,000 in 1913. This incredible growth was due primarily to immigration. Immigrants of German, Scandinavian, Russian, Polish and Ukrainian decent had arrived in huge numbers. These immigrants and much of the city's working class had settled in the north end of Winnipeg, leading to a diverse range of culture and religion in the area. In contrast, the city's ruling elite were exclusively Anglo-Saxon Protestants. These Canadian-born and British-born citizens had settled in the south end of the city, in areas such as Armstrong Point and Crescentwood. Margaret found a website on Armstrong Point homes and she was able to find the dates that homes had been built. As her parents had said, their house had been built in 1913. A large percentage of the homes in the area had been built from

1901 to 1913. The website also had information about the original owners of each home as well as the fact that until 1910, Middle Gate had been called Central Avenue and East Gate and West Gate had been called Assiniboine Avenue. By the time Margaret went to bed, she had decided she would do her essay on someone from one of the families who had lived in the area in the early 1900s.

CHAPTER 2

Tuesday, September 24, 2024

The alarm on Margaret's phone went off at 7 o'clock. She got ready for school and headed downstairs for breakfast. Both her parents were in the kitchen.

"Good morning," said her mom and dad.

"Good morning," said Margaret.

"Do you need a ride to school?" asked her mom. Her parents drove to work together. Her mom was an engineer and her dad was a lawyer. Their offices were both in downtown Winnipeg, so it was easy for them to drop her off at school, on their way to work, but many mornings she preferred to walk the fifteen minutes to school.

"Thanks, but I'll walk. I had some thoughts about my essay last night and I think walking would be helpful."

"OK. We'll see you later then," said her dad.

On her way to school, Margaret studied many of the homes. She had gone past them so many times over the years but had never really paid attention to them. Some of the homes were quite spectacular, even in 2024. So, imagine what people had thought of them in the early 1900s. She stopped in front of a house five doors down from hers. From her research the night before, she knew the house at 130 Middle Gate had been built in 1882. The houses on either side of it had been built in 1905 and 1906 and the two houses across the street in 1894 and 1909. She didn't know who had lived in the home at 130 Middle Gate when it was first built, but she planned to look that up later today.

When she arrived at school, Margaret headed to her locker. Realizing she was running a bit late, she quickly organized what she needed and hurried to Mrs. Sharpe's history class. She had just sat down at her desk as her teacher entered the room.

"Good morning, ladies," said Mrs. Sharpe. "Today, we're going to talk about the history of education in Manitoba and, in particular, the history of our school."

Margaret already knew some of the history of the school as she had learned it in earlier grades. She knew that Havergal College was a school for girls that had opened in Winnipeg in 1901 at 122 Carleton Street. It had been renamed Rupert's Land College in 1915. Riverbend School was opened in 1929, after Sir James Aikens passed away and gifted his house and grounds, on Westminster Avenue at Langside Street, to be used as a school for girls. By 1950, enrolment at both schools was decreasing so the two schools amalgamated to the Riverbend location and the new school was named Balmoral Hall (BH) School for Girls. What Margaret did not know was much of the history of Havergal College nor that of education, generally, in Manitoba in the early 1900s.

Mrs. Sharpe explained that prior to 1916, there was no compulsory school attendance in Manitoba. As such, the age a child went to school and what grades they were in, at each age, were somewhat different than present day. At Havergal, Kindergarten was open to children between six to eight years olds. Boys were allowed to attend Kindergarten and Form I, though right next door to Havergal was Tuckwell's School for Boys. Havergal did not use the term Grade instead the term Form was used. Girls continued through from Form II to Matriculation II which would allow for entry into university. Classes in the early 1900s included cooking, sewing, French, German, Art and painting. In the higher forms, there were courses in Latin, Mathematics, Literature and Science. The options for university study for women in the early 1900s were predominately teaching and nursing. However, some women did enter other fields of study and, in fact, the first female physician graduated from the University of Manitoba in 1892.

Mrs. Sharpe ended the class with a summary of what Winnipeg would have been like in the early 1900s. She discussed the booming population, which Margaret had read about the night before. While many people, in certain neigbourhoods, were leading successful, prosperous lives, there was also overcrowding and abject poverty in other areas, particularly in the north end of the city. Aid for the poor did not come from the government, it came from churches and charitable organizations. Government attitude toward the poor was often negative or condescending. Officials and wealthy citizens had an idealistic vision that anyone willing to work hard was bound to prosper and that poverty resulted from a moral failing on the part of the poor. So, while the wealthy lived an affluent and protected existence, they were often willfully ignorant of how harsh it was to be poor.

At the end of the school day, Margaret changed from her uniform into jeans and a sweatshirt, and she pulled her long brown hair into a ponytail. She wanted to be comfortable for her walk home as she was going to take a better look at the old house that had caught her attention that morning. She put her homework and textbooks in her backpack and left for home. It was a pleasant walk. The temperature was nice for a fall day.

When Margaret got to the house at 130 Middle Gate, she stopped to take a closer look. Removing her phone from her pocket and putting her backpack onto the sidewalk, she took a few pictures of the house, the neigbouring homes, the houses across the street and a view up and down the street. As she was taking the pictures, she decided she would write her essay on someone who had lived in that house in the early 1900s. Feeling happy with her decision, she put her phone back into her pocket. As she bent to pick up her backpack, she suddenly felt unsteady. The ground was shaking under her feet. Then she heard a loud explosion and she was thrown to the ground. While she was falling, she thought she saw houses disappearing around her. When her head hit the sidewalk, everything went black and she lost consciousness.

CHAPTER 3

"Hello? Hello? Are you all right?" a voice was saying.

Margaret slowly opened her eyes and there was a young woman kneeling beside her.

"Oh, you are awake. Can you hear me?" asked the woman.

"Yes. What happened?" asked Margaret.

"I am not sure. I was in my house and I happened to look out the window just as you fell. I came out to check if you were all right," said the woman. "Are you? Do you need help?"

"My head hurts but otherwise I think I'm OK." Margaret felt her head and noticed her ponytail had come undone and her hair was loose around her shoulders.

"OK?" the woman asked and looked confused. Margaret noticed what the woman was wearing, a white blouse and a long grey skirt. Her blond hair was long and pulled back with a pale pink ribbon. She wore no make-up and looked to be about Margaret's age but seemed older because of the clothes she was wearing.

"I'm fine. I should be able to walk home myself if you can give me a hand to stand up," said Margaret.

The young woman helped Margaret up and then asked, "Where do you live?"

"Oh, just five or six houses down the street." But, as she pointed in the direction of her home, Margaret noticed there were no houses in that direction. There was only the house in front of her and the one across the street. Then she noticed that although they were standing on a sidewalk, it looked different and so did the road. The material they were made from looked wrong.

"Where are the houses? What happened to the road? Where am I?" Margaret was confused and felt a rising sense of panic.

The young woman looked at her and said calmly, "The houses are here. The road is right there and nothing has happened to it. As to where you are, you are in front of my home on Central Avenue."

Margaret was not really listening to what the woman was saying. Instead, she said, "This makes no sense. I live on this street. Where did my house go?" Margaret began to cry.

The woman said, "My name is Charlotte Barbour. Would you like to come inside with me and we can try to figure out what happened?"

Margaret nodded. She had no idea what was happening, but she felt she could trust Charlotte and she knew she needed help.

Charlotte helped Margaret pick up her backpack and they walked toward the house. Once inside, Margaret knew there was a problem. Charlotte directed them through the front entranceway, past a huge wooden staircase and into the living room. But it did not look like any living room Margaret had ever seen. It looked like one from an old movie. The furnishings were all antique. There were armchairs, tables and a sofa but nothing looked modern. There was also an odd odour. It smelled like smoke and oil. The curtains on the windows were heavy, velvet drapes. The carpet was thick wool and dark red in colour. There was an upright piano, two china cabinets and a large fireplace.

Margaret sat down on the sofa and Charlotte sat beside her. Another young woman entered the room. She was wearing a long black dress with a white apron and a white cap on her head.

"Hello, miss. Will you and your..." the woman paused as she looked at Margaret, "guest be wanting some tea?"

"Yes, Ellen, tea would be appreciated," said Charlotte. Ellen left the room.

"Well now,"" said Charlotte. "How about we start with your name?"

"Oh, yes, my name is Margaret. Margaret Spears."

"And you live on this street?"

"Yes."

"That is interesting as I know all the names of the families that live on Central and Assiniboine Avenues and I do not know the name Spears. Though, there are some new homes currently under construction. Is your family to be moving here in the near future?" asked Charlotte.

As Margaret heard the names Central and Assiniboine, a shiver went up her spine. Then she asked, "Charlotte, before I answer your questions, can I ask you a question and I know it might sound a bit odd but please answer me," Charlotte nodded. "What is the date?"

"It is Saturday, September 24," replied Charlotte.

"Saturday?" It should be Tuesday, not Saturday, thought Margaret and with that, she knew what to ask next. "What year is it?"

"The year? It is 1904."

CHAPTER 4

Margaret's brain was in overdrive. Was it really 1904? If it was, how was she supposed to get back to 2024? Why was this happening?

"Margaret? Are you feeling all right? You have turned quite pale? Do you need to lie down?" Charlotte asked with a concerned tone to her voice.

"Actually, Charlotte, I think that is an excellent suggestion. Could I lie down for a short while?"

"Certainly. You can rest in my bedroom. Come with me." As they stood up, Ellen entered the room with a tray.

Charlotte said, "Ellen, please take the tray up to my room. My guest, Margaret, is feeling unwell and needs to rest. I will take her to my room and we will have our tea there."

Ellen nodded and proceeded up the staircase with Margaret and Charlotte behind her. At the top of stairs, there was a large landing with numerous doors that opened into other rooms off the landing. Ellen entered one of the rooms and Margaret and Charlotte followed. The room had a large bed, two comfortable armchairs with a table between them, a desk and a large fireplace. Ellen placed the tray on the table and she left the room.

Charlotte and Margaret sat down. Charlotte poured tea from a silver teapot into two porcelain teacups. She put milk and sugar into each cup and handed one to her guest. Margaret put her backpack at her feet and took the teacup. After drinking some tea and eating a few of the cookies and scones that were on the tray, Margaret took a deep breath and prepared to answer Charlotte's questions. She realized she would have to tread carefully and watch her wording so that Charlotte would not become frightened. She was going to need Charlotte's help and she did not want to scare her. Margaret suddenly felt immense gratitude to her English teacher, Miss McLennan, for assigning so many 19th century novels to read last year. She knew she would have to change some of her speech patterns and word choices to conform to 1904.

"Charlotte, I am quite confused as to how I came to be here but now that you tell me it is 1904, I have an idea of what might have happened."

"All right," said Charlotte. "Will your answers also explain why you are dressed so peculiarly? I did not want to bring it up, at first, but your clothing is not quite befitting of a young lady. You seem to be around the same age as me, but I know I have never seen a girl wearing the clothes you are wearing."

"You are correct, Charlotte. I will explain my clothing. And yes, I think we are around the same age. I'm seventeen. How old are you?"

"I, too, am seventeen," replied Charlotte.

"OK," Margaret took a deep breath and continued, "Charlotte, my name is Margaret Jane Spears. I live at 75 Middle Gate and I was born in Winnipeg on May 1, 2007." Margaret stopped talking and looked at Charlotte's face. She could see her new friend doing the math in her head.

"So, that means you are from 2024?" asked Charlotte.

"Yes. That is correct. This morning when I woke up, it was Tuesday, September 24, 2024."

"Extraordinary, you are from the future! Wait. Do you have a time machine?" Charlotte asked excitedly.

"How do you know about time machines?" asked Margaret.

"I have read *The Time Machine* by Mr. Wells. It was a marvellous book. Is it true? Are there time machines in the future? What is the future like? Is it like Mrs. Corbett's novel, *New Amazonia* and woman are in charge? Or it is like Mr. Bellamy's novels, *Looking Backward* and *Equality*, where everyone must participate in 'industrial service' and women can vote and wear pants? Please tell me that in 2024, woman can do more than just get married and have children." Charlotte was talking quickly and was clearly delighted with the news that Margaret was from the future. She leaned across the table and asked, "So, did you travel here in a time machine?"

"No, I did not come in a time machine. But you believe me?" asked Margaret. She had thought she would have to do more to convince Charlotte.

"Of course I believe you. You wear the oddest clothing, you carry a very strange looking rucksack and you use the term OK as if it were a commonly used word. It makes perfect sense you would be from the future," Charlotte responded. "So how *did* you get here? Were you hypnotized in a special sleeping vault? Did you hit your head?"

"What? Oh, are those ways that people time-travel in the books you've read?" asked Margaret.

"Yes."

"Well, I was not hypnotized, though I did hit my head when I fell. But I don't think that's how I got here," Margaret began. "Before I fell, I felt the ground shake and there was a loud explosion. As I was falling, I actually thought I saw the houses around me disappearing so, I think I was already in 1904 when I hit my head. What do you remember seeing when you saw me in front of your house?"

"Well, I did not see where you came from. As I passed the window I saw you on the sidewalk. I did not feel the ground move or hear any loud sound," replied Charlotte.

"OK. Oh. You said that is not a commonly used term. Should I not use it? What does it mean?" asked Margaret.

"It means, all correct, the same as you are using it. But it is a slang term and not really used in polite conversation."

"OK, so no more using the word OK!" smiled Margaret. Charlotte smiled too. "I need to figure out how I got here and how I'm going to get home."

"We will figure that out together, but first, we need to think of an explanation of why you are here in our house. My parents are at a garden party and they will be home later this afternoon. That gives us a few hours to come up with a story for how and why you are here, and find you some more appropriate clothing," said Charlotte.

23

CHAPTER 5

It took the new friends some time to come up with a plausible story, but eventually they felt their explanation would convince Charlotte's parents to allow Margaret to stay in the house. Charlotte found suitable clothing for Margaret and helped her get dressed. She showed Margaret how to pin up her hair and how to put on a hat. A proper lady had to pin her hair up after the age of fifteen and wear a hat out in public.

"I cannot believe how many layers of clothing you have to wear," said Margaret. "And these corsets really are as uncomfortable as I have read about."

"Well, at least your hair and clothes are now suitable for a woman in 1904," smiled Charlotte.

As Margaret had been getting dressed, Charlotte had told her about her parents and her life in Winnipeg. Charlotte's father, Thomas, was a lecturer at the University of Manitoba. His parents had immigrated to Canada, from England, in the 1850s and they had lived in Kingston. When they both passed away, Thomas moved to Winnipeg where he met and married Charlotte's mother, Emily, in 1885. Emily had come from a wealthy background. Her parent's had emigrated from Ireland, where each had grown up in privileged homes. Once married, and after a few years of travelling and living abroad, Emily's parents settled in Winnipeg in the 1850s. Her father started a carriage business. The business had done well and by the 1880s, Emily's older brother, William, had begun working there. Both of Emily's parents died just after Charlotte was born and Emily inherited a large sum of money. It was around that time that Emily and Thomas purchased their home in Armstrong Point.

"Do you have any brothers or sisters?" asked Margaret.

"No," replied Charlotte. "Do you?"

"No, I don't have any siblings either," said Margaret. Then she asked, "So, what else about you? Do you go to school?"

"Yes, I graduated from Havergal College this past June and I am planning to start at the University of Manitoba next month," stated Charlotte.

"Wait. Did you say Havergal College? The school on Carleton Street next door to Tuckwell's School for Boys?" asked Margaret.

"Yes. Is Havergal still a school in 2024?" exclaimed Charlotte.

"In a manner of speaking. The school I currently attend was once called Havergal College. It no longer has that name, nor is at the same site, but it does have Havergal's history. In fact, the school's current location is very close to here. Just over at the corner of Langside and Westminster," stated Margaret.

"I do not know of a street called Westminster, but I do know of the Aikens family property on Langside. Does that become a school? When does that happen?

What is the new name?" asked a very interested Charlotte.

Margaret started to feel a bit uneasy. How much should she tell Charlotte about the future? She was no expert on time travel, but she knew enough about science fiction to realize it was important not to tell people from the past too much about the future. She could risk changing the future for both herself and Charlotte.

"Charlotte, it would seem I should be careful as to how much I tell you about the future."

"Why? I really want to know about the future."

"I can appreciate that but if I tell you too much, it could change both of our futures." Charlotte looked confused, so Margaret continued. "I know this doesn't make a lot of sense to you and it doesn't to me either. But I do think it would be best if you don't know too much about the future. If I tell you too much, it might change decisions you are supposed to make in your future and then that could change my future. So, I think anything I say about the future should not be too specific. I also think I should limit the number of people I have contact with in 1904. When we figure out how to get me back to 2024, you're going to have to explain what happened to me and the fewer people I have had contact with the easier it'll be for you."

"You are correct that I do not fully understand why I can't know about the future, but I will respect your decision to temper what you tell me. And I also agree that you cannot meet too many people. But may I, at least, ask you a few important questions? I understand you are under no obligation to answer them..." she paused, "though I do hope you will." Margaret nodded. "Can women vote?"

"Yes," replied Margaret.

"When does that happen?"

"I don't think I should tell you the exact date, but it will be soon enough," said Margaret.

"What does that mean? In the next year, 5 years, 10 years, 20 years?" asked Charlotte.

"It's not next year and it's in less than 20 years," smiled Margaret.

Charlotte sighed and said, "Fine. I have one last question. Is it still the primary expectation for a woman to get married and have children or do we have more options than that?"

"Women can do much more than get married and have children. They can have careers, in any profession a man can have, and if they wish to marry and have children they can continue to work in their chosen profession," replied Margaret.

"Wonderful," smiled Charlotte.

There was a knock at the door and Ellen entered. "Miss, your parents are home and are asking for you," she said.

"Thank you, Ellen. We will be down in a moment." Ellen nodded and left.

"Are you ready with your story?" asked Charlotte.

"As ready as I'll ever be," replied Margaret.

CHAPTER 6

"Hello, Charlotte, and who is this with you?" asked her father, cordially, as Charlotte and Margaret entered the living room.

"Hello, Mother and Father. This is Margaret, Margaret Young. Margaret, these are my parents, Thomas and Emily Barbour. Margaret arrived from Toronto by train today and had a difficult trip. I am hoping we can help her."

"Hello, Margaret," said Mrs. Barbour. "Perhaps we should all sit down and then you can explain about your day." Mrs. Barbour gestured towards the sofa and armchairs and all four of them sat down.

Margaret began to tell the story she and Charlotte had devised.

"Thank you, Mr. and Mrs. Barbour. Charlotte has been ever so helpful to me today. You see, my aunt is Mrs. Edward Abbott."

"Oh, the Abbott family from across the street?" asked Mrs. Barbour. "Yes, I recall that Ada's maiden name was Young and I think she was originally from Toronto."

"Yes," said Margaret.

"Are they not away travelling in Europe until next month?" Mrs. Barbour asked.

"Indeed. It is interesting you were aware of that fact, as my parents and I were not. We thought the family was returning to Winnipeg in early September. My father and Aunt Ada are siblings. She and Uncle Edward had agreed that I could come and stay with them for a few months. There is so much talk of how quickly Winnipeg is growing that I thought I should come and see it for myself. So, I took the train from Toronto and arrived earlier today. Unfortunately, my luggage was misplaced during my journey and the man at the train station was unsure when it will arrive. I took a cab to my aunt and uncle's home but when I arrived no one answered. I did not know what to do next and I became quite upset. Charlotte saw me faint outside their house. She came out to assist me and brought me into your home. She has kindly given me some clothes to wear and I am hoping I can stay with you until my aunt and uncle return."

Charlotte's parents looked at one another and nodded. "Yes, that is a fine idea," said Mr. Barbour. "But you will need to telephone your family to let them know of the change in your plans."

"My parents and I had already made a plan. I am to contact them tomorrow so they will know I have arrived," said Margaret.

"We can telephone your parents tomorrow, after church, and then I can speak to them as well and let them know you will be staying with us until your aunt and uncle return. I will also call the railway station to inform them that when your luggage is found it should be delivered to our home," said Mr. Barbour. Margaret nodded but knew she would have to find a way to keep

Mr. Barbour from making any phone calls tomorrow. She and Charlotte would need to discuss a plan for that later.

"Well, now that all that is settled, we should tell you about the party," said Mrs. Barbour.

"My parents were at a garden party hosted by Mr. and Mrs. John Mills," Charlotte said to Margaret. Then she looked at her mother and asked, "Was it enjoyable?"

"Yes, we had a lovely time. Many people asked about you, in particular, Henry," said Mrs. Barbour with a smile.

"That is nice," replied Charlotte. She turned toward Margaret and said, "Henry is the Mill's eldest son. We met a few months ago...well, that is not exactly accurate. We have known each other since we were children because our mothers have been good friends for years. He is two years older than me and already attending the University of Manitoba. In June, he and I became reacquainted and now there are engagement rumours about us. I did not want to attend the party and have to make small talk all afternoon, so my parents allowed me to stay at home."

Charlotte gave Margaret a look that said she did not want this train of conversation to continue. Margaret recalled the comments Charlotte had made earlier about women, marriage and children and realized this was a personal matter for Charlotte. She would wait for her new friend to decide how much she wanted to share on this topic.

"The Mills have invited the three of us to dinner on Thursday and I accepted the invitation," said Mr.

Barbour, looking at Charlotte. "Perhaps some decisions can be made that evening."

"Fine," said Charlotte, looking down at her lap.

Ellen entered the living room and indicated dinner was ready. Mr. and Mrs. Barbour stood up and began walking toward the dining room. Charlotte and Margaret followed behind.

After dinner, Charlotte took Margaret upstairs to get settled in the guest room. Ellen followed behind with fresh towels for Margaret.

Once inside Margaret's room, Charlotte shut the door, turned toward Ellen and said, "Ellen, I would appreciate if you would not tell anyone about the clothing that Margaret was wearing when I brought her into the house earlier today."

"I will say nothing to anyone, Miss," said Ellen, adding more quietly, "but I did find the clothing she was wearing to be out of place?"

"Yes, Ellen, my clothing was out of place," said Margaret. "Did you think I looked like a young man?" Ellen looked surprised but she nodded. "Then my experiment worked!" exclaimed Margaret.

"Experiment?" Ellen and Charlotte said in unison.

"I have travelled by train, on my own before, and sometimes I have found myself a little uncomfortable as a *woman* travelling alone. Some men become quite forward and ask odd questions. I thought that I would dress as a man, on my journey from Toronto to Winnipeg, to see if I was treated differently. And I was. No one bothered me and if my luggage had not been misplaced, I would have been wearing appropriate clothing when I arrived."

"Well, your story is safe with me," said Charlotte.

"And with me as well," said Ellen with a nod. "The bed is already made up. Let me know if there is anything else you will be needing."

"Thank you, Ellen," said Margaret. Ellen smiled and left the room.

"Thanks for going along with my story. I was making it up as I was talking," laughed Margaret.

"Well done. I could never have come up with a story so quickly," replied Charlotte. "Now, we need a plan for the telephone calls tomorrow. Obviously, my father cannot make those calls."

Charlotte came up with an idea. In the morning, she would tell her parents that Margaret was feeling tired and unwell after several days of travel. She was not up to attending church with them. When the family returned home from church, Margaret would let them know she had already called her parents as well as the train station. If Mr. Barbour asked why she had not waited for him to be present before making the call, since he had wanted to speak to her parents, she would say that she had remembered her parents had a church picnic to attend after Sunday's service and that they had asked her to call them before they went to church.

"Well, you came up with a good plan for me," said Margaret, "and now I think I need to get some rest. But, before I do, can I ask one more thing?" Charlotte nodded. "Can you show me the bathroom?" Margaret had been a bit nervous as she wasn't sure what to expect of early 1900s plumbing. She was pleasantly surprised to find the bathroom looked almost the same as 2024. There was no shower but there was a large bathtub, sink, flushing toilet, and hot and cold running water.

With plans for the next day made, Charlotte and Margaret went to bed.

CHAPTER 7

Sunday, September 25, 1904

The next morning, Margaret stayed in bed listening to everyone else moving around the house, while they were getting ready for church. Ellen brought her a breakfast tray of eggs, toast and tea before leaving with the family for the Sunday service. The night before, Charlotte had mentioned her family attended Holy Trinity Anglican Church. Margaret knew the church; it was still there in 2024. Margaret's family attended All Saints Anglican Church, but she had been to Holy Trinity.

When the house was quiet, Margaret got up and decided to go for a walk. She needed to find a way to get home. Once she had dressed, done her hair and put on a hat, she found her backpack. Yesterday, after she had changed into clothing "befitting a woman of 1904," she had put all her own clothing and her phone into her backpack. She had turned off the phone to conserve its batteries. She now took out the phone and turned it on. The screen displayed Wednesday, September 25, 2024. With no network to connect to, the phone still thought it was 2024. It was a small link to home and it made Margaret smile. How strange it was to be without her phone or access to the internet. She knew she spent far too much time on it and thought she should try to enjoy this pleasant break from technology. Still, she slipped it into the pocket of her skirt thinking maybe she could take some pictures while out for her walk.

It was a sunny and pleasant morning as she began to walk down the street. She quickly realized how much space there was between the houses. Some of that space was taken up by gardens and lawns but some of it was also quite wild, filled with bushes, tall prairie grasses and small trees. It felt more like a rural setting than being in the city. Then she heard the rhythmic clatter of wheels on pavement and she looked up to see a horse-drawn carriage coming down the street. There was a couple in the carriage and they waved as they rode by. Once they had passed, Margaret took out her phone and took a few pictures of the street. As she walked back toward the house, she began to think about how she might get home.

She stopped in front of the Barbour's house, at the exact spot on the sidewalk where she had arrived yesterday and looked around. She waited to see if she would feel any shaking or hear any loud explosions. But all she heard was the wind in the trees and birds chirping. She took a deep breath and sighed. When she had first woken up, she had briefly thought that maybe she was just having a long, complicated dream. But she knew this was real. It was 1904 and she needed to find a way home to 2024. But, for now, perhaps she should try to enjoy being 120 years in the past. She walked back into the house and sat down in the living room.

As she considered what to do next, the family returned from church.

"Hello, Margaret. We were sorry you could not join us at church, this morning, though it appears you might now be feeling better?" said Mrs. Barbour. "Would you care to join us for lunch? Ellen has gone to help Mrs. Phillips to serve it."

"Thank you, Mrs. Barbour. I am sorry I could not attend church this morning, but I am feeling much better. I really needed a good rest. I have just been for a walk and would love some lunch," replied Margaret.

"Wonderful, it should be ready shortly," said Mrs. Barbour as she and her husband walked back toward the front door to remove their hats and coats.

Margaret looked at Charlotte and asked, "Who is Mrs. Phillips?"

"She is our cook. Her husband is our groomsman. They do not live with us as Ellen does, but they come daily," replied Charlotte.

"So, you have *three* servants?" asked Margaret.

"Yes, though I am sensing you do not have servants," said Charlotte, removing her hat and coat and placing them on a chair.

"No, we do not."

"I understand. I know that not everyone in Winnipeg has servants and I suspect there will be a time when we will not have them either."

"Charlotte, it is almost like you can see into the future," smiled Margaret. At that moment, Ellen entered the room to say lunch was ready.

Over lunch, Margaret explained to the Barbour's that she had already spoken with her parents and with the railway station. They seemed content with her explanation and did not ask any further questions on the matter, much to Margaret and Charlotte's relief. As lunch was ending, Charlotte asked if she could take Margaret for a ride around the city and her parents agreed.

Upstairs getting ready for their outing, Margaret asked, "Where will we be going? Am I dressed suitably?"

"I'm going to take you to meet a few of my friends for a picnic in the park and the clothes you are wearing are entirely appropriate for a Sunday drive. Though, I will find you a newer style hat." Charlotte handed Margaret a pale-yellow hat with a blue ribbon around the band. It matched well with the light blue skirt she was wearing. Charlotte chose a light pink hat for herself, which complimented her floral skirt.

Once ready, they went outside and Margaret followed Charlotte toward the garage. As they got closer to the structure, Margaret realized it was not a garage but, in fact, a stable. Mr. Phillips was there and he was bringing out a horse and hitching it to a buggy.

"So, you are going to drive us in this?" asked Margaret.

"Certainly, what did you think we would be taking?" Then Charlotte smiled. "Ah, you thought we would take an automobile. I suppose those are quite common in...." Charlotte caught herself before saying "the future" and instead said, "Toronto, but we do not have too many here in Winnipeg, as yet."

"Hmph," grumbled Mr. Phillips. "Those confounded contraptions are too loud and they scare the horses."

"I agree, Mr. Phillips. I am quite content with our fine horse, Nutmeg, and a buggy," said Charlotte.

Mrs. Phillips came out of the house carrying a picnic basket which she placed into the back of the buggy. Charlotte thanked her.

Once Nutmeg was harnessed and the buggy ready, Margaret and Charlotte climbed in and started down Central Avenue. Margaret was excited to see 1904 Winnipeg. She noticed at the end of the street there was a signpost indicating Cornish Avenue. And at the next intersection, another sign indicating Langside Street. These were the same street names as in 2024.

"I don't need to tell you about this property," said Charlotte, as they travelled along Langside.

Margaret shook her head and smiled as they passed the location that would one day become her school. There was a stone and iron fence around the property, though it was much lower than the fencing in 2024. Around the large home were beautiful gardens, trees and a meticulous lawn. The property looked both familiar and totally different all at the same time.

As they continued along Langside, Margaret noticed there were numerous homes under construction. Instead of cement sidewalks, there were wooden boardwalks on each side of the road and many elm trees growing along the street. The trees were much smaller than in 2024 and looked newly planted. Charlotte noticed Margaret staring at the trees and said, "To beautify the city, the municipal leaders decided to plant elm trees throughout the city. The elm tree was chosen because it is native to this area and can tolerate Winnipeg's harsh climate. Apparently, they will grow quite large and will eventually create a beautiful canopy over the street that will also provide shade from the sun in the summer. Does that happen?"

"Yes, it does," Margaret replied with a smile. "In 2024, there are many beautiful, large elm trees that grow along numerous streets in Winnipeg. I didn't appreciate how long ago those trees were planted. It's nice to see them here."

When Charlotte turned the buggy onto Broadway Avenue, Margaret was truly astonished. The homes along Broadway were enormous. They travelled past All Saints Anglican Church and Margaret observed that, in 1904, it was not yet a stone church, instead it was made of wood. They crossed Osborne Street and Margaret noticed how wide the street was and that the boulevard in the centre of Broadway was adorned with trees and flowers.

Charlotte stopped the buggy and pointed out some landmarks. "You can see the streetcar railway lines down the middle of the boulevard and all the overhead wiring for the electric streetcars. I like riding on Broadway because the streetcars and the roads are separated, which is not the case on Main Street. It doesn't matter quite so much today as the streetcars do not run on Sundays. Over there, you can see the Fort Osborne barracks and that is Government House, the home of our current Lieutenant Governor, Mr. McMillan. And there is the Legislative Building. Premier Roblin was elected last year."

"Roblin? Premier Duff Roblin?" asked Margaret.

"Duff? No, his given name is Rodmond. Who is Duff Roblin?"

Oh no, thought Margaret. Duff Roblin was the Premier of Manitoba who had been responsible for building the Red River Floodway, known as Duff's Ditch, but it wasn't built until the late 1960s. If he was related to Rodmond Roblin, thought Margaret, he would likely be his grandson.

"I've accidentally given you some information about the future. There will be another Premier Roblin, later this century."

"Interesting, is there anything else you want to share about politicians who are related? Will there be Prime Ministers who are father and son?" Charlotte laughed.

Margaret laughed too but said no more on the topic. Charlotte pulled the reins to get Nutmeg moving again. She pointed out the Land Titles office and the University of Manitoba. When they got to Carlton Street, Charlotte stopped and pointed out her school, Havergal College.

"If you look on the other side of Carleton Street, do you see that large, red-stone house with the enormous front porch?" asked Charlotte.

Margaret smiled and replied, "I know that house. It was the home of Hugh John Macdonald. He was the son of Canada's first Prime Minister, Sir John A. Macdonald." In 2024, the home was a museum, which Margaret had visited on a school field trip last year.

"Well, in 1904, it *is* the home of Hugh John Macdonald. His son, Jack, is at university with Henry.

I have been to the house a few times. It is quite lovely." Margaret nodded in agreement.

As they continued along Broadway, Charlotte commented on the Strathcona Block apartments as well as the newly built Manitoba Club and the Old Fort Garry Gate. What really struck Margaret was how many of the buildings they passed were still standing in 2024.

At the end of Broadway, across Main Street, there was a large wooden building. "That is the Canadian Northern Railway depot," said Charlotte. "It is not nearly as impressive as the new Canadian Pacific Railway station on Higgins Avenue."

When they turned onto Main Street, Margaret really felt like she had stepped into a history book. The street was wide. The electric rails ran down the centre of the street and horse-drawn buggies, wagons and carriages moved up and down the street, along the sides. Margaret could not figure out how people knew where to drive. There were no traffic signs or traffic lights and it seemed people just rode wherever they wanted. A large wagon, pulled by four horses, passed by them. On the side of the wagon was written, "The Arctic Ice Company" and there was a painted picture of a polar bear standing on an iceberg.

Margaret asked, "Is there ice in that wagon?"

"Yes," replied Charlotte.

"You can make ice in 1904?" queried Margaret, slightly confused. She was fairly certain there had been no refrigeration or ice-making capabilities in 1904.

"What do you mean *make* ice? Ice is cut from the frozen river in the winter and stored in icehouses filled with hay and sawdust. It is delivered to people's homes as they request it. Can you make your own ice in 2024?" Margaret nodded and thought about how many modern conveniences she just took for granted.

At the corner of Main and York Avenue, there was a large three-storey building with flags on top of it. As they rode by it, Margaret could see signage that said, "Hudson Bay Store." She was surprised to see a Bay store on Main Street. She thought it had always been on Portage Avenue.

At the same intersection, Margaret noticed another large building. Charlotte said, "That is the Assiniboine Block. It was an apartment building, but it's now being renovated into a new hotel. I believe it will open next year and be called the Empire Hotel."

As they continued along Main Street, Charlotte said, "That is the Fortune Building." Margaret thought the three-storey brick building looked familiar and was sure it was still there in 2024. The signage on the building showed it was a Real Estate office. Margaret also noticed there were many buildings under construction. Charlotte stopped in front of one of the buildings which had scaffolding all around it.

"That is the Scott Block and it is going to be a new store called Scott Furniture. It should be open by the end of this year," said Charlotte.

When they reached the intersection of Portage Avenue and Main, Charlotte stopped the buggy. She pointed to a large three-storey building a short distance down Portage Avenue and said, "That is the Queen's Hotel. It is currently being renovated inside as it is fairly old. It should reopen by next summer." On another corner of the intersection, Margaret could see a large five-storey building with signage indicating it was the "Canada Life Assurance Company."

As Margaret looked westward down Portage Avenue, she noticed how distinctively different it looked in 1904 than 2024. There were no skyscrapers. The tallest buildings were three storeys and most were only one or two storeys high. She was sure she could see open prairie in the distance. She thought of the cemetery she had visited a few days earlier and realized that in 1904, it would have been well outside of the city limits.

Suddenly, there was an incredibly loud noise as a motor car drove right past them. It was travelling much faster than any of the horse-drawn transportation and kicked up a lot of dust from the road. Margaret realized that, in comparison, the clip-clop of the horses' hooves was quite pleasant and she understood why Mr. Phillips did not like the sound of motor cars.

As they continued along Main Street, they passed by the Merchants Bank and looking down McDermot Avenue, Margaret could see the newspaper buildings of the Winnipeg Tribune and the Manitoba Free Press. There was also a bright blue building, called The Blue Store, which seemed to be a clothing store. Margaret saw the Post Office building and more banks: the Royal Bank of Canada, the Bank of British North America, the Bank of Hamilton and the Eastern Townships Bank. She was sure a number of the buildings they passed were still there in 2024. There were many other businesses as well: horse stables, jewellers, barristers, pawn brokers, dentists, photographers, electricians, chartered accountants and even an orthopedic surgeon advertising artificial limbs. There were brick buildings, wooden buildings and many new buildings under construction. There were Union Jack flags hanging on almost every block. Margaret was amazed at how busy the street was. Not only were there bicycles, buggies, wagons and horses on the roads, but there were also lots of people walking on the sidewalks. There was a real feeling of energy and excitement.

When they got to William Avenue, Charlotte stopped the buggy and said, "Let's get out here for a short walk."

Charlotte pulled the buggy to the side of the road and they got out. As Charlotte tied Nutmeg to a post, Margaret could smell a uniquely strong odour. She looked around her and noticed a large amount of horse manure on the streets. She had not smelled it as the buggy was moving but now that they had stopped, the odour was quite pungent. She followed Charlotte who walked toward a small garden in front of an enormous and quite ornately trimmed brick building. Margaret had seen pictures of the building and knew it was the old Winnipeg City Hall, though in 1904, she supposed it was not yet that old.

They sat down on a bench in the garden and Charlotte pointed to a ten-storey building on William Avenue. "That is the Union Bank Building. It has just been built and it is reportedly the tallest building in Canada and the second tallest building in the British Empire." Margaret recognized the building. It was still there in 2024.

Charlotte turned toward the building behind them and said, "And this is City Hall. It is actually our second city hall. The first one was completed in 1876, but it was built on a creek bed, so it became badly damaged due to the settling of its foundation. It had to be torn down in 1883. This new building was constructed in 1886 and is often referred to as The Gingerbread City Hall."

Margaret laughed as she looked at the building, "It does look like a Gingerbread House. I have to ask; how do you know so much about the history and architecture of the city?"

"My Uncle William, my mom's brother, is somewhat of an amateur architect and historian. He finds everything about Winnipeg's past, and its present, quite fascinating. At family dinners, he likes to regale us with stories he has learned about the newly constructed buildings or past events that happened in the city. Not everyone in my family appreciates his stories but I really do and I have been trying to pass on some of that information to you, while we are riding through the city."

"Well, you most certainly have done that," replied Margaret. Then as she turned toward the fountain located in front of City Hall, she noticed two familiar sights. "Is that the Boy with the Boot statue and the Queen Victoria monument?"

"Yes. Are those still there in 2024?" asked Charlotte.

"They are not in front of City Hall anymore, but they are in a beautiful garden in an enormous park. I love to go for walks in that garden with my grandmother and we often stop to admire the statue and the monument. It's amazing to see them here." From her many visits to the English Gardens, in Assiniboine Park, Margaret knew neither the park nor the gardens had existed, in 1904, so she did not refer to them by name.

Charlotte nodded, smiled and then said, "Before we continue our ride, I have something I want to tell you. I'd like to talk to you about Henry."

"All right," replied Margaret, "I'm listening."

CHAPTER 8

Charlotte began her story. As she had told Margaret previously, she and Henry had known one another since they were young, as their mothers were friends. During their childhood, they saw one another at various social functions but as they got older, they did not really interact at those functions, instead spending more of their time with their own friends. Once Charlotte had finished school and was given some more freedoms, such as taking the buggy for a drive on a Sunday afternoon, she and her friends had started spending time with Henry and his friends. Over the summer, they had begun sharing picnics together and going to fairs, amusement parks and the beach. Over those months, Charlotte admitted she had become quite fond of Henry and she believed he felt the same way. She explained that her parents were quite openminded and even though the prevailing social expectation was that a young women should marry and have children, her parents knew she wanted to go to university and pursue a career of her own. But Charlotte also knew, once she married, she would be expected to stop working to be a wife and mother. She had expressed these concerns to Henry and he supported her aspirations. He did not want to marry anytime soon, though he was interested in marriage one day, and had even told Charlotte he should like to marry her. The problem was with Henry's family. His father ran a successful grain company and assumed Henry, as his eldest son, would finish university and then begin working in the family business. But Henry's dream was to become a lawyer and while the University of Manitoba did offer a three-year reading course in law, which along with articling could allow for entry into the legal profession, it was not as highly regarded as an actual law degree. Henry wanted to go to Toronto to obtain a law degree, but his parents did not support this plan. In fact, they were the ones pressuring him to marry Charlotte, as that would mean he would stay in Winnipeg and work in the family business.

"Well, that is quite a dilemma," said Margaret, "what are you and Henry going to do?"

"We do not know. We decided to enjoy our summer and delay thinking about it but now that fall is here, we know some decisions need to be made. That's what is going to be discussed at the dinner at Henry's home later this week." Charlotte sighed, "Thank you for letting me tell you all that. I appreciate you listening to me. But now, we need to continue our ride. We are all due to meet shortly." Charlotte looked at her gold wristwatch, which Margaret noticed looked like a miniature pocket watch attached to a gold bracelet. "Oh my, look at the time, we really do need to hurry up."

Margaret and Charlotte walked back to the buggy and continued down Main Street. Charlotte pointed out the police station. Margaret was thinking that in 2024, that was where the Centennial Concert Hall was located. At the corner of Main Street and Rupert Avenue was a large building with the name "Brunswick Hotel" on its facade. Margaret did not recognize that building. Charlotte turned the buggy onto Rupert Avenue and started down toward the Red River. As they rode, Margaret could see an entrance to a park. It was green and lovely and a much-appreciated reprieve after the busyness of Main Street.

"This is Victoria Park," said Charlotte, as she stopped the buggy. They got out and Charlotte tied Nutmeg to a post with a water trough. She removed a blanket and the picnic basket from the buggy and they walked into the park. It was full of people. Most were either standing or sitting on the grass in front of a large wooden structure that looked like a gazebo.

"Wonderful, there they are. They got a great spot near the bandstand," said Charlotte, as she walked toward a group of people who were smiling and waving at her.

"Wait," said Margaret, "that is quite a few people. What if they ask me things and something I say changes the future?"

"I don't think that is going to be a problem. Once I've introduced you, they won't ask you too many questions. Really, most of them are here because they want to do the talking," smiled Charlotte, "you'll see. It will be fun. I promise." Margaret followed Charlotte toward the group.

"Hi, Charlotte. Great to see you," said one of the girls. There were four girls and five boys standing and talking together. They all turned toward Charlotte and Margaret.

"Hi, everyone. I would like you to meet a friend of mine. This is Margaret. She is visiting from Toronto and is staying at my house. Margaret, these are my friends, Alice, Gertrude, Martha, Lucy, Stuart, Billy, Jack, Charles and Henry." Margaret smiled at all of them.

"Hello, Margaret," they all said in unison.

"Thank you, it's nice to meet you all," replied Margaret.

Charlotte's friends helped her spread out the blanket and take the food out of the basket. As Margaret watched the group, she noticed a distinct difference in the clothing worn by Charlotte, Alice and Gertrude compared to Lucy and Martha. The first three wore brightly coloured dresses that had embroidered skirts. Lucy and Martha had plain beige blouses and light grey skirts made of a coarse looking material. It was similar with the young men. Jack and Billy's clothing was more loose fitting and looked like it was made of a much rougher material than any of the other three. There were also patches on the elbows of their jackets. Margaret had the distinct feeling that Jack, Billy, Lucy and Martha did not live in the same neighbourhoods as the others. But they were clearly all friends.

"You must be wondering how we can all possibly be friends," smiled Billy. "It's obvious we didn't all go to school together or live on the same street."

"Yes, how did you all meet?" asked Margaret. She was interested to hear how they knew one another.

"We all met here at the park, but not exactly at the same time," said Charlotte.

"Charlotte, Alice and I went to Havergal together," said Gertrude. "And over the summer, we started coming to the park with Stuart, Henry and Charles. That's when we met Lucy and Martha. Then shortly after, they introduced us to Jack and Billy."

"Here's a rundown on all the lads," said Henry. "Charles and Stuart are chums of mine and we are at university together. Stuart is a bit of a local celebrity. He's a member of the Winnipeg Shamrocks Lacrosse team that won the gold medal at the Olympics, this past July, in St. Louis. Charles is a good friend who wants to be a lawyer, as do I, so we get along great. Billy, works for his father who runs a general store over on Selkirk Avenue and Jack works in the carriage business that is owned by Charlotte's uncle."

"We all laughed when that connection was made. It's a small world, but that's Winnipeg!" remarked Charlotte. Wow, thought Margaret, she had had the same thought a few days ago, while talking to her mom and grandmother.

"Lucy and Martha work at a garment factory. And they live in the same neighbourhood as Jack and Billy," finished Charlotte.

"And you all meet at this park on Sundays?" asked Margaret.

"Yes, because unlike my finely dressed friends here, the rest of us only have one day free from work, each week," laughed Jack. Everyone smiled at Jack's remark.

The group sat down on the blankets and began eating what they had brought: sandwiches, pretzel-shaped bread with butter and jam, dumplings, perogies and fruit. Biting into a white, glazed cookie Margaret thought was shortbread, she was surprised to taste peppermint and a hint of lemon. Noticing Margaret's odd expression, Martha asked, "Do you like that?"

"Yes, it's wonderful. I thought it was shortbread because it looks like the cookies my Nana makes."

"My Oma made these. They are peppermint cookies. She normally only makes them at Christmastime, but it was my cousin's birthday yesterday and she really loves these cookies. So, my Oma made a big batch and there were some left for me to bring today," explained Martha.

Margaret tried all the different foods and everything was delicious. She took a sip of the drink in front of her and was startled to find it was whiskey. It made her start to cough.

"Do they not drink whiskey in Toronto?" asked Charles, with a smile.

"I'm sure they do, but probably not in a public park," Charlotte quickly replied for Margaret. Margaret nodded as she coughed.

"Well, if my mother and her Woman's Temperance group have their way, no one will be drinking or having fun ever again," announced Alice. "They really think that alcohol is responsible for all of society's ills. Poverty, poor sanitation, slums, prostitution, it is all to be blamed on alcohol. If there was no alcohol all those things would magically disappear. It makes me so mad. There is no acknowledgement that it is they, their husbands, and all the other wealthy people in this city, that have contributed to those social problems and that giving large sums of money to charities does not absolve them of their part in the problems." Everyone was quiet for a moment and then they all burst out laughing.

"So, now that Alice has got things started, does anyone else want to speak up?" asked Henry.

Charlotte looked at Margaret and said, "This is the part we all love. The discussion of real issues. Most of us live a sheltered and protected existence and we're not supposed to talk about such things. Adults just want us to talk about topics they want to hear about and we have to agree with their opinions. It is so much better to talk among friends, where you can say what you think. Would you agree?"

"Yes, I would," replied Margaret, thinking to herself how much she really liked Charlotte and her friends.

CHAPTER 9

The group of friends talked about a myriad of topics including politics, religion, unions, women's suffrage, immigration, urban growth and hospitals. Margaret could hardly keep up with all the conversations. These were young people who believed passionately in their convictions. All of them, the young women *and* men, believed that women should be able to vote. And they all had their own aspirations and goals. Jack wanted to run his own business. Charles and Henry did not want to work for their fathers. Lucy wanted to be a teacher and Charlotte wanted to get a science degree.

As they were talking, a sound began to grow in the distance. It was a train and it became louder as it got closer to the station, which Margaret knew was a few blocks away on Higgins Avenue. She could hear the wheels on the tracks, the chugging of the steam engine, the train whistle and the sound of the brakes as it stopped at the station. She could also see dark, black smoke rising in the distance and there was a distinctive smell of burning coal. Margaret coughed as the soot wafted over the park and she could feel it landing on her skin and tasted it in the air. Once the train had stopped at the station, it was not quite as loud.

"Never been to a park so close to a train track?" asked Billy.

"No, it's quite loud and I'm surprised the soot can reach us," said Margaret.

"Actually, this isn't so bad. We're a good distance away from the station. Where I live, I can see the tracks from my house," said Jack. Lucy, Billy and Martha nodded in agreement. "We just learn to tune out the sound and we get used to soot covering everything in our north end neighbourhood."

At that moment, a new sound began. It was music.

"Great, the band is starting. Let's dance," said Stuart. The whole group jumped up and moved to an area closer to the bandstand where other people were beginning to dance. Margaret remained seated on the blanket.

"Are you coming with us?" asked Charlotte.

"In a few minutes. I think I'll just sit and watch for now," replied Margaret.

"OK," smiled Charlotte and Margaret laughed.

On the bandstand, there were three musicians: one man on a piano, another playing a fiddle and a third man playing a banjo. The music was incredibly energetic. Margaret felt it was familiar and she thought it might be called "ragtime." As she watched everyone dancing, she realized no one seemed to care that some of the women were dressed in elegant skirts and blouses while some of the men were in plain grey pants with suspenders. They were all there to dance and enjoy themselves. When Margaret saw Charlotte and Henry dancing together, she reached into her pocket and pulled out her phone. She carefully hid it behind a picnic basket so no one could see and she took a few pictures and some video of Charlotte and Henry. As she placed her phone back in her pocket, Billy walked toward her.

"Would you like to dance?" asked Billy.

"Yes, I would, though I'm enjoying watching everyone having fun. You all seem like such good friends," replied Margaret.

"We are and I know it probably looks odd, to someone from Toronto, that people like Henry and Charlotte would associate with people like me, Jack or Lucy."

"Looks can be deceiving," replied Margaret.

"Yes, they can," smiled Billy. "Charlotte, Henry and their friends are great people. We all think quite similarly on many topics and we all like spending time together. I don't know if we will remain friends. It has been a wonderful summer and now it's fall. And once winter comes, I don't think we will be meeting here very often and who knows what we all will be doing by next spring. But, for now, we will just enjoy every Sunday afternoon we can, together."

"Well said. All right, I'm ready to dance but I'm not sure I'll know the steps," said Margaret.

"Steps? There are no steps, just dance whatever way you want to," smiled Billy, as he took Margaret's hand and headed towards the others dancing.

When the band finished, the group went back to sit on their blankets. They ate the remaining food and then began packing up to leave.

Martha asked Margaret, "Did you enjoy your afternoon here in Winnipeg? I have never been to Toronto, but I imagine it is far bigger and better than Winnipeg."

"You know, I really had a wonderful time this afternoon. And yes, Toronto is bigger than Winnipeg, but I don't think it's better. Winnipeg is young and vibrant. Everyone knows one another. It's like a small town but it's a growing city. If Easterners are people who live in towns and cities east of Winnipeg and Westerners are people who live west of Winnipeg, then what is Winnipeg? I think it's both. It's like a large, established eastern city but it's new and untamed, like out west. And that's what makes Winnipeg amazing!" exclaimed Margaret.

"Wow, the government should use that in their immigration campaign," laughed Henry.

Margaret smiled, "Really, thank you all for letting me join you today."

As they left the park, the friends stopped to say goodbye to one another. While several got onto horses or into buggies and carriages, Margaret noticed that Jack, Billy, Lucy and Martha did not have any transportation and were heading home on foot.

Henry was the last one to say goodbye to Charlotte and Margaret. He said to Margaret, "It was very nice to meet you and I hope to see you again while you are here visiting."

"I hope so too," replied Margaret. Though, she was not sure she would see him again.

He turned toward Charlotte and said, "I had missed seeing you at my parents' garden party yesterday, but I am glad I saw you today. I know you and your parents are coming for dinner later this week but maybe I can see you before that?"

"That would be nice. Please feel free to visit in the next few days," replied Charlotte.

"I will do that," said Henry, as he got onto his horse. Then he, Stuart and Charles rode away and Charlotte and Margaret started on their way back to Armstrong Point.

CHAPTER 10

"Did you really enjoy yourself or were you just being polite?" asked Charlotte, as they rode back along Main Street. "I think there must be far more exciting things to do in 2024."

"You know what, Charlotte, there really isn't. Hanging out with friends is not that different in 2024, than in 1904. My friends and I like to talk, listen to music and dance. And we like to drink, sometimes, but not whiskey," laughed Margaret.

"What did you think of Henry?" asked Charlotte.

"I think the more important question is, what do you think of Henry?" retorted Margaret.

"Yes, I know I need to decide what to do but I would like to hear your opinion," replied Charlotte.

"Well, I think he, and all your friends, are wonderful people. They were all so welcoming and friendly. I felt very comfortable with them. But what I noticed most about Henry is the way he looks at you."

"Looks at me, what do you mean?" asked Charlotte.

"He looks at you like a man totally besotted!"

"Besotted...hmm...like Mr. Darcy in *Pride and Prejudice*?"

"Yes. You can tell Henry is very much in love with you. He listens to everything you say and is always smiling when he is around you. And, by the way, it's the same when you look at him," replied Margaret.

"What? Really? I look besotted?" exclaimed Charlotte.

"Yes, you do," replied Margaret.

"I really do care about him. I find him incredibly handsome and so very intelligent. He knows so much about *everything*. He even finds all my uncle's discussions of history and architecture as interesting as I do." Charlotte stopped talking and then grinned, before saying, "I suppose I am a woman besotted." Margaret raised her eyebrows and nodded.

Charlotte continued, "I do want to marry Henry, but just not now. I know that is what Henry wants as well. I just don't know what his parents are going to say when we tell them our plans do not involve marriage for a number of years."

"I really think you and Henry know best and as long as you make these decisions together, it will all work out," said Margaret giving Charlotte's hand a gentle squeeze.

"Thank you, Margaret. I can't believe we only met yesterday. I feel I have known you for ages and that we are kindred spirits."

"Me too," agreed Margaret.

Charlotte didn't say anything else and Margaret could tell she was thinking. Margaret began thinking too. She thought about 2024 and 1904. She thought about how many of the buildings she saw in 1904 were still there in 2024. It was a testament to the people who had constructed them and the vision they must have had for Winnipeg. She thought about the people she had met that day. Charlotte's friends were not that different from her own friends. They wanted to have fun, but they also knew they had a future in front of them. One where they would need to make choices and decisions about what they wanted to do with their lives and who they really wanted to be. Then a comforting thought came over her. If she did not find a way back to 2024, she knew that she would have friends here. But that saddened her, too, because she already missed her family and friends so much.

"You look sad, Margaret. What's the matter?" asked Charlotte.

"I was thinking of my family and my friends and how much I miss them. I want to go home but what if I can't get back to 2024?"

"You're going to get home," said Charlotte, with confidence. She smiled as she recited, "I am no prophet, but I assure you that she will not be away much longer, for she is a woman of such resource that even though she were in chains of iron she would find some means of getting home again."

"Huh?" asked Margaret, confused.

"Sorry, I was trying to be clever. That was my version of a passage from the *Odyssey*," replied Charlotte.

"The…what?" asked Margaret, still confused.

"Charlotte pulled on the reins to stop the carriage. She looked at Margaret and said, "The *Odyssey*…" Margaret's face still had a blank expression, "by Homer."

"Oh, is that the one about Achilles and the Battle of Troy?" asked Margaret, remembering an old movie she had watched with her mom and grandmother. They had both loved the actor who played Achilles and she recalled them telling her the movie was based on a poem by Homer.

"You're close. That's Homer's other poem, the *Iliad.* The *Odessey* is about the King of Ithaca, Odysseus, and his epic journey home after the Trojan war."

"So, you were trying to say I'm like Odysseus and I'm on my own epic journey to get home," asked Margaret.

Charlotte started the carriage moving again. Realizing that her reference to Greek literature had been lost on a girl from 2024, she sighed and said, "It would probably have been simpler if I had just said, 'let's not think like that and as much as I really like having you here, I do want you to get home." Margaret laughed and nodded in agreement.

CHAPTER 11

"Good evening, Mother and Father," said Charlotte, as she and Margaret entered the dining room. Mr. and Mrs. Barbour were already seated. Margaret saw a familiar selection of food on the table. It was a Sunday roast beef dinner, complete with mashed potatoes, gravy and Yorkshire pudding.

"Good evening, girls," said Mr. Barbour, as Margaret and Charlotte sat down. Mr. Barbour said grace and then began to carve the roast beef. As plates of food were passed around the table, Margaret took time to look around the dining room. She had been so tired the previous night she had not really noticed her surroundings. The room was beautiful. There was a chandelier above the table. Its four lights emitted a soft yellow glow that highlighted the wood ceiling and gave everything in the room a golden hue. There were two large sideboards on either side of the room and many elaborate paintings and portraits on each wall.

"Did you have a nice ride this afternoon, Margaret?" asked Mrs. Barbour.

"Yes, thank you, Mrs. Barbour. Charlotte took me for a lovely ride through the city and then we went to Victoria Park for a...picnic." Margaret hesitated as she was unsure if Charlotte's parents knew about their meeting with friends and the dancing.

Mr. and Mrs. Barbour laughed. "A picnic, you say?" asked Mrs. Barbour, "I hope there was time for music and dancing, too?"

"My parents know about my friends and our outings on Sunday afternoons. They are quite supportive. I think sometimes they are a bit envious and would like to join us," smiled Charlotte. Mr. and Mrs. Barbour smiled too.

"Margaret, what did you think of the young people of Winnipeg you met today? Were they what you expected, coming here from Toronto?" asked Mr. Barbour.

"They were all wonderful, Mr. Barbour. I thoroughly enjoyed meeting them. We discussed such interesting topics and of course, the food, music and dancing were great fun," replied Margaret.

"Ah, the discussions, Charlotte has told us of those," said Mr. Barbour, "What topic interests you the most? Do you support voting rights for women, like Charlotte?"

"Well, yes, Mr. Barbour, I do. But I'm not too concerned about the right to vote. I know it will happen."

"You do?" exclaimed Mrs. Barbour. "When do you think it will happen?"

"I do not *think* it will happen; I *know* it will happen."

"Well, if you are not concerned about women's suffrage, because you know it is inevitable, then what topic of discussion do you find most interesting?" asked Mr. Barbour.

"I find technology fascinating. All the inventions of the last century were considerable: typewriters, sewing machines, electric lights, the telephone, photography, and, of course, the automobile and now, the airplane."

"The airplane? Do you mean that engine powered glider invented by the two American brothers? I read that they were successful in flying it last December but could not repeat it this spring. Do you think that invention will work?" asked Mr. Barbour.

"I do and I also think, in this century, there will be many more inventions and I am very much looking forward to seeing them all," replied Margaret.

"I like your optimism for the future. Certainly, reading many of the current newspapers, one might feel more defeated than cheerful," said Mr. Barbour.

"Well, I don't believe everything I read," said Margaret.

"I imagine you don't," laughed Mr. Barbour. The others laughed as well.

"This is so great," said Margaret, "I love this kind of dinner conversation. It reminds me of home."

"Are you missing your parents?" asked Mrs. Barbour.

"A bit, but I will be home soon enough," said Margaret. She realized she didn't want Charlotte's parents to ask too many more questions about home because she did not want to become upset in front of them.

Charlotte sensed Margaret's discomfort and changed the topic by asking, "Margaret, how do you think we could decide on what inventions will be the most important in the 20th century?"

"I propose that I return to Winnipeg, for dinner with you all, at some point in the future. Then we can discuss what new inventions we have found to be the most interesting," replied Margaret.

Mr. Barbour lifted his glass and said, "Well then, a toast...to the future."

"To the future. Cheers," everyone said, as they tapped their glasses together.

After dinner, Ellen and Mrs. Phillips came in to take away the dishes. Mr. Barbour began talking to Charlotte as the two of them walked toward the living room. Mrs. Barbour stepped beside Margaret and the two of them followed Charlotte and her father.

"I am very glad you are here, Margaret," she said.

"Thank you, Mrs. Barbour, I am glad to be here too. I do not know what I would have done if Charlotte had not helped me and I am so grateful to you and Mr. Barbour for allowing me to stay in your home."

"Of course, but what I meant is that I am glad you are here for Charlotte. I am not sure how much she has told you about Henry," inquired Mrs. Barbour.

"She has told me enough that I realize she and Henry have some important decisions to make," replied Margaret.

"Yes, they do and those are their decisions to make. Though in the last few weeks, I have sensed a great deal of trepidation from Charlotte and I was becoming concerned. She has talked to me a bit, but I knew there was more. Perhaps she has been able to share some of her feelings with you, as she now seems more content. She was so happy at dinner. It was lovely to see her more like herself, so I want to thank you, Margaret."

Mrs. Barbour put her arm around Margaret's shoulder and gave her a small hug.

The four of them sat and talked in the living room for a short while. Then Charlotte excused Margaret and herself and the two girls headed upstairs.

"Do you have any thoughts on how you might get back to 2024?" asked Charlotte, once they were in Margaret's room.

"No, I don't and I am too tired to think about it now. Can we work on a plan tomorrow?" asked Margaret.

"Certainly," replied Charlotte. "Have a good sleep and I will see you in the morning."

"Good night, Charlotte. See you tomorrow," said Margaret.

CHAPTER 12

Monday, September 26, 1904

When Margaret and Charlotte went downstairs for breakfast, Mrs. Barbour was already there, finishing her meal.

"Your father has gone to work. What will you girls do today?" Mrs. Barbour asked Charlotte.

"I'm not sure. I thought we might take a streetcar to River Park," replied Charlotte. "What do you think, Margaret."

"That sounds nice," Margaret said. She had never been on a streetcar.

"Yes, that does," said Mrs. Barbour. "You are also welcome to join me at Mrs. Mason's. A few of the ladies and I are playing tennis this morning."

"The Masons have a large river property on Assiniboine Avenue. They had a tennis court built in the spring and have been inviting friends and neighbours to play. My mother particularly enjoys tennis," said Charlotte. "Thank you, but I think we will decline, and Margaret and I will have our streetcar outing."

"All right," said Mrs. Barbour as she got up from the table, "Have a good day and I will see you both for dinner."

When Mrs. Barbour had left, Margaret asked, "Where is this River Park we are going to?"

"It is on Osborne Street at Jubilee Avenue. It is a nice park…but that is not where we're going," replied Charlotte.

"Where are we going then?" asked Margaret.

"We're going to the North End," replied Charlotte. "Since meeting Lucy, Martha, Jack and Billy this summer, I have wanted to see where they all live, but neither Alice nor Gertrude has wanted to go there with me. As much as they like meeting up with the others on Sundays at Victoria Park, neither of them wants to see that neighbourhood. They have been told by their families that it is a dirty, unsafe place to be and they are not allowed to go there."

"And you want to go there?" asked Margaret.

"Yes, I do," said Charlotte, "I thought you would want to see it as well."

Margaret was thinking about Charlotte's description of Winnipeg's North End and how a similar description was still used to describe it in 2024. She realized that she and her friends had never gone to the North End and they did not know anyone who lived there. Margaret began to feel unsettled. Why did she know so little about the North End? At least here, in 1904, she had actually met people who lived there. Margaret answered Charlotte with conviction, "Yes, I do!"

After breakfast, as the girls were leaving for their streetcar outing, Henry rode up on his horse.

"Good morning, Charlotte and Margaret. After such an enjoyable afternoon yesterday, I thought I would come and see you both today. You look like you are about to leave? Where are you going?" asked Henry, dismounting his horse.

"I am taking Margaret on a streetcar ride," replied Charlotte.

"I would think that, coming from Toronto, you have ridden on streetcars before," said Henry. Then with a knowing look he said, "You're going to go to the North End, aren't you?"

"Yes, we are," Charlotte replied intently, "Margaret wants to see it too!"

"All right. But if you must do this, may I accompany you?" asked Henry.

Charlotte looked sternly at him. She had asked Henry to go along with her to Winnipeg's North End before. He had said he would but somehow, he never got around to it. She knew he had been procrastinating and didn't want her to go to that part of the city. But now he was offering. She knew it was a good idea for Henry to go with them and she realized she wanted him to come. Her face softened and she replied, "Yes, that would be fine."

"I would suggest you both change into clothing that is a little more..." Henry trailed off.

"A little more, what?" demanded Charlotte, looking down at her own outfit and then at Margaret's. She had selected a light green skirt for herself and a pale yellow one for Charlotte. They wore white blouses, and jackets and hats that matched their skirts. "I think we look lovely"

"Yes, you do. But I think you would be best to wear clothing that is a little plainer, simpler, older, perhaps…We will stand out a bit in the North End and your clothing will make that even more pronounced," finished Henry.

"Oh. Thank you. We will go inside and change," replied Charlotte.

"I am going to take my horse to Mr. Phillips and I will meet you here when you are ready," said Henry.

Charlotte and Margaret changed into long dark skirts, cream-coloured blouses, less stylish jackets and simple grey hats. Charlotte affixed a flower to each hat to "add some colour" she said.

Henry was waiting on the front step and they started walking down Central Avenue toward Sherbrook Street. At Cornish Avenue and Assiniboine, Margaret expected to see her local library but when she instead saw a building with a sign that read, "Winnipeg Water Works," she recalled the library was not built until 1915. Margaret could see the Maryland Street Bridge. It had metal trusses on the sides and streetcar tracks running down the centre. On the other side of the bridge, Margaret could see St. Mary's Academy. At the corner of Cornish and Sherbrook, they stopped to wait for a streetcar. Margaret saw a large three-storey wooden building across the street, where the present-day Misericordia Health Centre was located.

"That is the Winnipeg Maternity Hospital. It was built a few years ago by the Misericordia Sisters to help unwed mothers," said Charlotte.

"Only unwed mothers can have babies there? What about married mothers?" asked Margaret.

Henry and Charlotte looked bewildered and then Charlotte replied, pragmatically, "They have their babies at *home*. The maternity hospital is a place for an unmarried woman to go when she finds herself in a difficult situation. She can stay there until she has her baby and then the sisters will help her put the baby up for adoption." Margaret wanted to ask more questions, but the tone of Charlotte's reply made it clear that, in 1904, this was not a topic for further discussion.

A streetcar arrived. It was wood panelled with a sign on the side, near the top, that said "Sherbrook Street." On the lower portion, "Winnipeg Electric Railway Company" was painted in yellow. Glass doors opened once the streetcar stopped and the three stepped in. Henry paid their fare. There were a few people already sitting inside the streetcar, but it was not full. As they sat down, the streetcar began to move and the driver rang a bell.

Charlotte turned to look out the window and Margaret took the opportunity to talk to Henry. She told him the story about herself that she had told Charlotte's parents. He told her about his parents and his three siblings. As he had mentioned at the park, he wanted to study law, but his father wanted him to work in the family grain business. As Margaret listened, she realized Henry was a good man and she could see why Charlotte liked him. When they finished their conversation, Charlotte began to talk with Henry and Margaret took the chance to turn and look out the window.

When the streetcar approached Portage Avenue, the driver rang the bell and stopped to allow other streetcars, wagons and carriages to go by. Margaret heard multiple bells ringing from different streetcars. She still wondered how people knew when to stop or go, but she was grateful they all seemed to know what they were doing. On the corner, Margaret saw a large four-storey stone building with a turret and a cross on top. There were many children playing on the front lawn of the building and some adults who looked like they were supervising the children.

"What is that building?" she asked Henry.

"That is the Manitoba Institute for the Deaf and Dumb," he replied. "My parents know the principal of the school and his wife. She is a teacher at the school and is partially deaf. The school is widely regarded and there are students from Manitoba, Ontario, Saskatchewan and even British Columbia."

Next to the institute was a fire hall and across the street was a three-storey building with a sign that said, "McCullough Drug Store." Margaret was sure the same building was still there in 2024. Travelling down Sherbrook, there were a number of small homes and some two-storey buildings that Margaret thought could be apartment blocks. There were also numerous businesses and a few banks. As they crossed the intersections at Ellice and Sargent Avenues, some of the buildings, on the corners, looked familiar to Margaret. When they crossed over Notre Dame Avenue, Margaret looked westward and she could see a large park on the south side of the street and on the north side, several taller buildings a few blocks down.

"Those buildings are the Winnipeg General Hospital and the Medical College," said Henry, "Also, the street we are on was called Sherbrook Street back there, further south, but now that we have crossed Notre Dame, the same street is called Nena Street. Street names that change, as you travel along them, are common in this city. It is somewhat annoying and makes it difficult to give directions, but that's Winnipeg."

They exited the streetcar at Logan Avenue and Henry said, "This is as far as it goes. We will have to walk to the Salter Street bridge to cross over the railway yard into the North End."

The yard was on Higgins Avenue, which was two blocks away, but they could already see, hear and feel the trains as they walked toward the bridge. The rumbling and shrieking of the trains was incredibly loud. On the other side of the tracks, Margaret could see numerous warehouses and factories. There were also many smokestacks billowing out dark, black smoke. As they approached the bridge, it was obvious it was quite old and in poor condition. There were no streetcar lines on it but there were pedestrians and wagons crossing it.

"How old is this bridge?" asked Charlotte.

"It was constructed at this location in 1898, but it is actually the original Main Street bridge, which was built in 1881. When they built the new Main Street bridge in 1897, they moved the old bridge here to create an overpass for the railway yard. It does need to be replaced but there is discussion of a new Brant-Brown overpass being built just west of here, so this bridge will likely be demolished," replied Henry.

Margaret knew the bridge they were on was still there in 2024, though it had been rebuilt and renamed the Slaw Rebchuk bridge. She wondered if the Brant-Brown Overpass was what was now called the Arlington Street bridge. She knew it would not be constructed until 1912 because in November 2023, after 111 years of use, the Arlington Street bridge was finally shut down due to corrosion and safety concerns.

Once they started walking across the bridge, the sounds from the trains seemed quieter. Now, they could see hundreds of men walking toward the boxcars and eventually gathering in groups around each one. Henry explained that they were inspection and sampling crews with the Board of Grain Commissioners. Each grain car was sealed by a station agent at its originating location. Once the car arrived at the Winnipeg yard, the seal was broken by a board employee and the contents were sampled. Then, the car was resealed. Next, the bags containing grain samples were taken to the board's office for completion of paperwork. The bags were then taken to the inspection department, at the Grain Exchange Building, to be graded. A certificate indicating the grade was given to the owner of the grain so he could receive payment. Crews worked 24 hours a day, 7 days a week. It was hard work being on a sampling crew.

As they got to the other side of the bridge, Henry announced, "Ladies, welcome to the North End."

CHAPTER 13

They began walking down Salter Street away from the railway yard. As they walked, Margaret became aware of some new odours. There was still the smell of the railway but there was also an earthy, putrid odour. As they approached Jarvis Avenue, Henry stopped and asked Charlotte, "You are sure you want to do this? I have been here several times this summer, to meet with Jack and Billy, and they have shown me around and parts of what you will see are not pleasant."

"And you couldn't bring me on any of those visits?" asked Charlotte.

"Well, no, I really did not feel you should be here," said Henry.

"Well, you were wrong, I do want to be here. How am I to know what is happening in my own city if I do not see it for myself?" replied Charlotte.

"All right," said Henry. "And Margaret, you want to be here too?"

"Yes, I do," said Margaret, though she felt a little nervous.

They began walking and within a few moments, Margaret understood what Henry had warned them about. The dwellings they passed were shacks made of wood boards, paper and metal. There were dozens of women and children outside each shack. All of them were dirty and skinny. Most of the children had no shoes and their clothes were so thin they looked transparent. There were also animals. Cats, dogs, hens, roosters and Margaret even thought she saw a cow. The smell was overwhelming.

"There is no running water or sewage connections here, so the toilets behind these dwellings are outhouses. The worst ones are the box closets as they use a box, instead of a pit, and their contents often overflow and drain into the street. As well, the outhouses are shared by multiple homes," said Henry. "As you can imagine, this leads to the spread of diseases, such as typhoid fever."

Then they heard yelling, "No, no, do not take them." A woman was holding a small child, and there were five other children around her. All the children looked sickly and had visible sores and cuts on their arms, legs and faces. The hair on their heads was covered in a thick substance. A well-dressed man said, "We must take them to the hospital. They are covered in lice and scratching the bites has led to serious wounds. These children need to be treated."

"Should we stop and help?" asked Charlotte.

"No, keep walking. There is nothing we can do to help," replied Henry. "The man with them is the doctor and he will make sure the children are taken to the hospital."

"Why would that woman not want her children to get treatment? They desperately need it. Did you see their hair? What was on it?" asked Charlotte.

"A home remedy for lice is to put lard grease on the scalp in hopes of suffocating the lice and nits off," said Henry.

"That doesn't work!" exclaimed Margaret.

"No, it does not," agreed Henry. "But parents would rather do that than have their children taken away to a hospital."

"But why?" asked Margaret.

"It is difficult for the people who live here. Many are from places where English is not their native language. They have different customs and beliefs than those who run the institutions, such as hospitals. They fear the unknown and are worried that if their children are taken, they will not be brought back," replied Henry.

"That is ridiculous, of course the children will be brought home after they are cared for in hospital," said Charlotte. "What type of government would allow children to be abducted from their parents? Certainly not in Canada."

Margaret said nothing. She knew that Charlotte and Henry would be unaware that, across Canada, Indigenous children were being taken from their families and put into residential schools. These schools were established by Christian churches and funded by the federal government with an aim to convert the children to Christianity, educate them and assimilate them into Canadian society. The residential school system was devastating to Indigenous children, as well as their families and communities, as they were forced to abandon their languages, traditional beliefs and cultural practices. Margaret could understand why the immigrants in the North End, in 1904, were sceptical of bureaucratic intervention.

They continued walking to another street. Along this one was a mixture of shacks and buildings that looked like houses, though many had poorly constructed extensions attached. Henry explained that as immigrants came to Winnipeg in such large numbers, there was not enough affordable housing to accommodate them. That led to the building of the slum dwellings they had just passed. Also, when inhabitants of houses in the area decided to leave and move to a different neighbourhood in Winnipeg, developers, seeking easy profits, would turn the home into a boarding house and rent out space in every square inch of the house. That led to more overcrowding and disease. And because more immigrants kept arriving and new houses were not being built, the cycle continued.

"But these people all have jobs, don't they? There is so much work to be found in Winnipeg," said Charlotte.

"That is true. Many of them have jobs but they are working for very low wages. The wages are not enough for them to live on or to raise a family. In many families, both parents have jobs and once children are old enough, they must get a job to contribute their wages to the household," stated Henry.

"Well, why aren't their wages higher? Shouldn't their employers pay them a decent wage?" asked Charlotte.

"They should. But that is also complicated. Many of their jobs are in industries controlled by businessmen, such as my father and his colleagues. As businessmen, they want to keep their costs down so they can earn a good profit. And even if one businessman wanted to increase wages for his workers, it is not always that straightforward," said Henry. Both Margaret and Charlotte gave him a confused look of "why on earth not?" "My father did try to increase wages for some of his workers but the objections from other men in the grain industry were so great, it was impossible for him to follow through with his plan."

The three were now at an intersection of a much wider street. "This is Selkirk Avenue. It is one of the main commercial streets in the neighbourhood. Billy's family store is along here and I thought we could go there next," said Henry. Margaret and Charlotte nodded.

Margaret noticed there were many different types of shops and buildings on Selkirk. She saw butchers, barbers, tailors, plumbers, blacksmiths, a fur store, a hardware store and several grocery stores. There were signs in the windows in so many different languages. They walked past a Catholic Church, a Presbyterian church and a synagogue. She also noticed how busy the street was. It looked similar to Main Street. There were lots of people walking on the wooden sidewalks, horses and wagons on the street and streetcars moving up and down the centre of the street.

Henry stopped in front of a two-storey building with a sign that said, "Fitzhenry General Store." When they entered, Margaret could not believe how many items there were in the store. There were goods on the floor, on shelves, attached to the walls and even hanging on hooks from the ceiling. She could see hats, lamps, clothing, shoes, fabrics, ropes, saddles, harnesses, pipes, and dishes. There were also various brands of foods: tin boxes of Blue Ribbon coffee and tea, burlap sacks filled with Ogilvie flour and oats, and glass jars of Blackwood Brothers vinegar. Margaret smiled when she noticed a large sign advertising Coca-Cola as delicious and refreshing.

"Hello, you three. Good to see you," said Billy, as they approached him.

"This is quite a store," said Charlotte.

"Thanks, the store is on the main level and we live on the second floor," said Billy. "My family is very proud of the store." A young man walked toward them. He looked almost identical to Billy; both were tall with red hair.

"This is my older brother, Sam. Sam, these are my friends. You know Henry," Sam nodded. "And this is Charlotte and Margaret. Charlotte and Henry have been friends since they were children, and Margaret is a friend of Charlotte's family and she is staying with them while she is visiting Winnipeg from Toronto."

"From Toronto and you're here in the North End?" asked Sam. "How did that happen?"

"Charlotte wanted to come here and I agreed. Henry was kind enough to accompany us and show us around," replied Margaret.

"Sam, can you come and give me a hand?" a woman called from across the store.

"That's our mother. I should go and check what she needs. Billy, go on outside with your friends, I can cover you for a bit," said Sam.

"Thanks, let's go," said Billy.

Once they were outside, Billy asked, "What have you seen?"

"We walked over the bridge and looked at the houses on Jarvis, Stella and Flora Avenues, just like you showed me," said Henry.

"And what did you think?" asked Billy, looking at Margaret and Charlotte.

"In a city as prosperous as Winnipeg, it is heart-breaking to witness such poverty and hardship. It is not right," said Charlotte. "Why doesn't someone help them?"

"Actually, this whole community tries to help. My parents have a credit system in their store for those that need it. People can pay it off in cash, with other produce or by labour. Other merchants in the community bring food and clothing to the neediest families," said Billy.

"I'm sorry. I did not mean to imply that you were to solve the situation, though I am glad to hear that people come together to help one another," said Charlotte.

"What of charitable organizations, do they not provide aid?" asked Margaret.

"They do. However, not without judgement," replied Billy, "Many of the missions that are meant to help the poor actually blame them for the conditions they live in. If a mother dies of consumption, instead of acknowledging that overcrowded housing and inadequate sanitation may have contributed to her death, it is said that it was her life of sin and drunkenness that caused her death. When people do ask for aid, they are made to feel it is their incompetence that led them to require aid. And even when assistance is given, it is minimal, because giving too much will result in the person shirking their responsibilities and continuing to live an immoral life. So, many people simply do not ask for aid as it only makes them feel worse and does not actually help their situation."

"But when people, such as my parents and their friends, give money to those missions, they assume it is helping the less fortunate. Is that not actually what happens?" asked Charlotte.

"Before I answer that, I want to make a comment on the people who give money to the missions. What I'm going to say may seem harsh, but I think it's important." Charlotte, Henry and Margaret nodded in agreement.

"The leaders of this city are wealthy, elite men. The city council and mayor are the ones who write the laws and run the city. They have civic budgets which they spend to provide services such as policemen, fire brigades, city parks and the construction of bridges and roads. They are also supposed to provide services such as sanitation and public health, but very little money is spent on those services because it does not affect them. They all live in their beautiful homes, socialize only with one another and give no thought to the serious social problems in this city. They make donations to charities so they can feel better about themselves. If they really wanted to help the people of the North End, they would."

Billy continued, "But to answer your question about those donations, I do not want to mislead you. They do go to the poor and not all organizations are run the way

I explained, but I am saying that sometimes there are conditions that make it difficult for those who need help to ask for it. And you also need to remember, many people are too proud to ask for or receive any assistance. They are hardworking people with jobs and they want to make their own way," replied Billy.

The four young people stood in silence for a few moments. They had similar thoughts. Poverty is a difficult situation. How do you "solve" it? There are many issues involved, including low paying wages, inadequate housing and poor sanitation. What really struck Margaret was that for all the technological and social advancements made over the next 120 years, many of the same problems still remained.

Billy broke the silence, saying, "I am very glad that you stopped in to see me while you were here. I should get back to work."

"Ladies, I think we should begin heading back home," said Henry.

Billy offered to take his friends to the streetcar stop on the other side of the bridge. He went into the store and came out in a few moments.

"My parents said I can take you in the store wagon." Billy gestured toward a wagon on the street with "Fitzhenry General Store" painted on its side. "Climb on in," he said.

Billy took them to the streetcar stop on Logan and they set off back to Armstrong Point. They chatted a little on the return ride, but they were mostly quiet, as they each reflected on what they had seen and learned while visiting Winnipeg's North End.

CHAPTER 14

When they arrived back at Charlotte's home, Charlotte and Henry went to the stable to get his horse. Margaret went inside and sat in the living room. Ellen brought in a tray of sandwiches and tea. Margaret stared at the food with a mixture of guilt and relief. She was hungry and wanted to eat but she knew others didn't have enough and for those people, hunger was an unending reality.

Charlotte entered the room. "Did Henry leave?" Margaret asked.

"Yes. I thanked him for going with us. He was concerned for our state-of-mind after what we witnessed today but I assured him we are both fine. Was I correct in saying that? Are you?" asked Charlotte.

"Yes, I am," replied Margaret, "though, I am a bit unsettled."

"I imagine so. In the novels I have read, they often reveal a utopian future where poverty and disease are eradicated. Is that the case in 2024?" said Charlotte.

"I wish I could say it is but, unfortunately, poverty and disease still exist," replied Margaret.

The girls sat quietly as they ate, both deep in their own thoughts. Eventually, Charlotte stood and retreated upstairs for some time alone.

Margaret continued sipping her tea. She looked toward the front window. The sun was low and shining directly into the living room. The velvet drapes were pulled aside but not fully. She noticed that one drape had two small tears in it and the sun shone through the cuts, illuminating a design on the far wall. As Margaret observed the pattern of alternating bright and dark lines projected onto the wall, she remembered an experiment from her physics class. The double-slit experiment demonstrated that light behaved both as a wave and as a particle. That experiment from the late 19th century, along with many other experiments and theories in the 20th century, eventually evolved into a branch of physics known as quantum mechanics. As Margaret stared at the pattern on the wall, an idea began to form in her mind about how to get home. She remembered she had her physics textbook in her backpack, so went up to her room to do some reading.

Margaret spent the next few hours reading and thinking. Eventually, she dozed off for a nap. It was 7 o'clock when Charlotte knocked on her door to let her know dinner was ready. Margaret put the pins that had fallen from her hair back into place and went downstairs. Charlotte and her parents were already at the dining room table.

"Good evening, Margaret," said Mrs. Barbour. After Margaret was seated, Mr. Barbour said grace and dinner began.

"Charlotte was telling us about your trip to the North End today," said Mrs. Barbour.

Margaret looked at Charlotte. "I told my parents the truth about where we went," Charlotte confirmed. "I said it was my idea and that you were hesitant but knew you wouldn't be able to change my mind. They are not angry but are glad that Henry went with us. I had just finished telling them about the streetcar ride and the walk over the bridge."

Charlotte told her parents about the dwellings and the people they saw. She also talked about Selkirk Avenue, Billy's family store and the discussions they'd had with Billy about charities and the poor.

When Charlotte had finished, her father asked, "How do you both feel after what you saw today?"

"I'm going to let Margaret answer that first, since I have been the one doing all the talking," replied Charlotte.

"I do not feel quite as optimistic as I did at dinner last night," began Margaret. "The situation is the same in...Toronto...but I, like Charlotte until today, have never been to that part of the city and so do not know what it is really like. Now that I have seen it here, I feel like I want to do something to make it better, but I don't know what that something is." Charlotte nodded in agreement.

Mr. Barbour said, "That is a perceptive statement from someone so young. Many people, much older than you, grapple with the same questions when it comes to social inequalities that result in poverty and illness and related issues of wages and housing. Change starts with being aware of the issues. And as your friend, Billy, observed, many of the upper class simply ignore these problems and conveniently blame the problems on the very people being affected because it eases their guilt. The fact that you both recognize and acknowledge the problems means you are open to looking for solutions."

"But what are the solutions? What can we do to make this better?" pleaded Charlotte.

"I wish I could give you short and simple answers to those questions, but I cannot. I know you want to make it better right now, but I do not think these are problems that can be solved quickly," replied Mr. Barbour.

"Why not?" asked Charlotte.

"There are many issues intertwined in the discussion of poverty. For instance, you might not realize how much education, or lack of it, can affect the prosperity and health of a community. I think there should be compulsory school attendance for all children from the age of six until at least fifteen. Being literate and educated helps everyone. People have access to better jobs which pay higher wages. And with regards to wages, I think there should be a minimum wage so that employers cannot underpay their workers. And finally, with respect to sanitation and health, there should be running water and sewage systems in all businesses and homes, and everyone should have access to proper medical care without worrying about how much it will cost."

"Those are all excellent ideas, so why doesn't someone make them happen?" asked Charlotte.

"No one person can do all that. It needs to happen over time," said Mr. Barbour. "Many of the policies needed to implement these ideas will need to come from municipal, provincial or federal governments. Voters will need to cast ballots for the men from political parties that promise to bring the ideas forward and..."

"Or *women*," interrupted Margaret. "Women will get the vote and that means that women will also, one day, run for office and be elected to positions where they can help make new laws. So, voters will cast ballots for the man or woman they feel represents them and their community."

Mr. Barbour looked approvingly at Margaret, "I hope that is one day the case. But all this will take time. While we agree that achieving universal suffrage, public education and health care, and fair wages for all workers are all commendable goals, not everyone thinks so. And for those who do, not everyone will agree on how to accomplish them. There will be disagreements and compromises may need to be made and all that takes time."

As Mr. Barbour was speaking, Margaret began to realize that is exactly what had happened over the past 120 years. All his ideas eventually happened, but they took time. New governments had to be elected, decisions had to be made, and policies and laws had to be written in order to accomplish adequate sanitation, compulsory education for children, universal health care, minimum wages and many other laws that benefited society. While poverty still existed in 2024, there had been significant improvements to many

Canadians' lives since 1904. That gave Margaret a bit of perspective. Societal changes take time. New policies and laws can only come into effect after much debate and discussion. If changes are made hastily and without good rationale, then unforeseen consequences could occur which might end up being worse than the original problem the change was trying to address.

"Thank you, Mr. Barbour. I now see this from a new perspective. We are in this for the long haul. We need to stick to our convictions, on what we want to see accomplished, but we also need to be patient. None of these issues can be solved by one person, it will take all of us, working together, to make the significant changes needed to help our society grow and flourish," said Margaret.

"Very well said, Margaret. We are in this for the long haul," replied Mr. Barbour.

The table was quiet for a moment and then Charlotte said, "I would like to say a prayer." Everyone stopped eating and bowed their heads and Charlotte began, "Loving God, we pray for everyone in our city who is living in poverty. Show us how to do our best to help them. We pray that you lift up their spirits and give them hope. Help them to know we care about them and pray for them. We ask this in the name of Jesus Christ our Lord. Amen."

"That was lovely, Charlotte. Thank you," said her mother. The others nodded in agreement.

The remainder of dinner was subdued but pleasant.

CHAPTER 15

After dinner, the girls went to Margaret's room and once inside, Charlotte asked, "Do any of the ideas my father mentioned actually happen? I know you said you can't tell me too much about the future, but I need to know something!"

"OK. I can tell you a few things. As your father was talking, I realized that all the things he mentioned will happen, but they will not happen at the same time. From my perspective, they have all happened and they all happened a long time ago. But from your perspective, they will happen over many years. Some might occur in the next few years, others will take decades, and still others even longer than that. Your father is right. Complicated social issues cannot be solved quickly."

"It does make sense that change takes time, but I also think there is more I could do now, or in the near future, to help. I am going to talk with my parents and Henry and come up with some ideas," said Charlotte.

Both girls sat quietly for a few minutes, then Margaret said, "On a different topic, earlier this afternoon, I did some...." She paused, momentarily, being about to say "reading" but realized she could not let Charlotte see a 21st century physics textbook, so she said, "…thinking and I may have a theory on how I got to 1904 and maybe it can help me get back to 2024."

"All right, what is your theory?" asked Charlotte.

"So, you know of the sciences, such as physics and chemistry?" asked Margaret.

"Yes, I have learned a bit about those subjects but that is why I want to study science at university, to learn more about them," replied Charlotte.

"Good. In chemistry, there is the periodic table of elements and those elements are made up of atoms," said Margaret. Charlotte nodded. Margaret continued, "and molecules are made of two or more atoms."

"Yes."

"And in physics, atoms and molecules are matter and have energy."

"Yes, that makes sense," replied Charlotte.

"Well, in 2024, there are concepts, in physics, know at quantum mechanics and quantum entanglement. Now, I know a bit about these from school, but I need to emphasize only a bit, so this is going to be my very simplistic overview of some very complicated physics. Quantum mechanics describes the probabilities that particular particles, like atoms, might behave in a particular way in a particular setting. Quantum entanglement involves a particular setting of two particles in which they could be located very far apart from one another. And when I say far apart, I mean way out in the universe, like to the Milky Way. Now, because these particles are entangled it means that if something happens to one of the particles, the other particle, even though it is so far away in space, will also be affected." Charlotte nodded. "So, what if instead of the two particles being separated by a great distance in space, they were instead separated by time. If something happened to a particle at one moment in time, could its entangled particle, at another point in time, be affected?"

"Could it?" asked Charlotte.

"That's the thing. There isn't an answer to that. This is all just a theory but maybe that is how I got here. Maybe there is an entangled particle, or particles or something else, here in 1904 that is connected to something in 2024, and I got caught up in that connection and I have been catapulted across time."

"Catapulted? That is an unusual word to use. You were like a projectile that was launched through time?" asked Charlotte.

"Maybe." Margaret had chosen the word "catapulted" because while reading her physics textbook earlier, she had recalled an analogy her physics teacher, Mr. East, had made during a lively class discussion about the possibility of time travel. He had said, "The catapult is quantum mechanics and the tension in the rope is entanglement."

"I also know that an enormous amount of energy was produced in the process of me travelling here, to 1904, because the ground shook so violently and I heard a thunderous sound, like an explosion when it all happened."

"It would make sense that a large amount of energy would be released if one was being catapulted across time," said Charlotte.

"I agree. But what do we do to get me back to 2024?" asked Margaret. The two girls looked at one another and were silent for a moment as they both thought about what to do next.

Finally, Charlotte said, "I think we should start by you remembering exactly what you were doing in front of my house before the ground started shaking. Maybe, there is a detail you can recall that will help us."

"All right let's try that. This is what I remember. On my way to school in the morning, I had passed your house and it had caught my attention."

"Why? In what way?" asked Charlotte.

"I was thinking that your house was one of the oldest homes on the block, having been built in the 1880s, and I was also thinking about how many people would have lived in it over all those years. So, on my way home from school, I stopped in front of your house, and I..." Margaret stopped before saying "took some pictures" because just like the physics textbook, she did not want to show her phone to Charlotte. She had no idea how she would explain that piece of technology. "...Imagined all the different people who could have lived in the house and then I made the decision that I was going to do my essay on someone who lived in the house in the early 1900s. That is when the ground started to shake, I heard an explosion and then I was here and met you."

"Hmm. What if thinking about all the different people who have lived here and deciding to do the essay on someone from the early 1900s, is what brought about the entanglement between the two particles, groups of particles or the 'something else' you referred to?" asked Charlotte.

"What do you mean?" asked Margaret.

"What if, the particles are related to this house, as it is in both 1904 and 2024. And what if, as you thought about the past inhabitants of the house, that changed the behaviour of the particle in 2024. Then the particle in 1904 was affected and, as you proposed, you were caught up in the entanglement of the two particles."

"And, if that was the case, then perhaps I could recreate that process by thinking of the inhabitants of the house in 2024 and that might change the behaviour of the entangled particle here in 1904. Then the entangled particle in 2024 would be affected and I might be able to go back to 2024."

"Why not? I like our theory!" smiled Charlotte. "When do you want to try it?"

"Tomorrow? Though, we will need to pick a time when there is less chance someone might see us. If it works, I do not want someone to see me vanish into thin air. Perhaps we can get up early tomorrow morning before anyone is awake and try it then," said Margaret.

"Ellen gets up around 6 o'clock and Mr. and Mrs. Phillips get here by 6:30. My parents are not usually up until about an hour later and I get up shortly after them. We could time it to try before my parents get up but after Ellen and Mr. and Mrs. Phillips are already at their work. Maybe 7 o'clock. The sun will be up by then. I do not think we want to do this in the dark."

"I agree, I would prefer to do this in daylight. I like your plan, but sunrise is not until after 7, so it will not be light enough then," said Margaret.

"No, sunrise is just after 6. It will be light by 7," corrected Charlotte. Margaret realized there was no Daylight Saving Time in 1904. While in September

2024, sunrise was after 7 o'clock, in 1904 it would have been after 6.

"I will set an alarm clock and come wake you at 6?" asked Charlotte. Margaret agreed.

They stayed up most of the night talking. Charlotte eventually went to her room so they could both get a little sleep. Margaret made sure to set the alarm on her phone for shortly before 6. She wanted to make sure she woke up on time and she wasn't sure how reliable a 1904 alarm clock would be.

CHAPTER 16

Tuesday, September 24, 1904

Margaret and Charlotte were both up and Margaret had dressed in her clothes from 2024.

"If this works, please know I am going to miss you very much," she said. "I am so grateful for all your help."

"I will miss you, too. I am so glad you arrived in front of my house. Thank you for meeting my friends, for listening to me and for going with me to the North End. I am really looking forward to the future, even though you couldn't tell me as much as I wanted to know," smiled Charlotte. "And don't thank me just yet. We still need to get you home."

They went quietly down the stairs and out the front door. The sun was up and there was no one on the street. The girls stood on the front step and hugged.

"I don't want to say goodbye. I want to imagine we will see each other again. Can we just say, take care until we meet again?" asked Charlotte.

"I like that. Take care, Charlotte, until we meet again."

"You too, Margaret. Take care, until we meet again."

Margaret turned and walked to the spot on the sidewalk where she had found herself three days ago.

Charlotte remained on the front step. Margaret closed her eyes and began to think of her parents. She waited a few moments, then opened her eyes. She felt nothing, no movement of the ground, heard no loud sound.

"It isn't working," she said turning back toward Charlotte.

"What are you thinking about?" asked Charlotte.

"My parents," replied Margaret.

"Remember, you said you'd been thinking about all the people who had lived in *this* house. "You need to think of *all* those people again," said Charlotte.

Margaret closed her eyes for a second time. Instead of thinking of all the people who *had lived* in the house from 2024 to 1904, she thought of all the people who *would live* in the house from 1904 to 2024, beginning with Charlotte and Charlotte's parents. As she opened her eyes, the ground began to shake and there was another very loud noise. Margaret stayed steady on her feet and watched as Charlotte disappeared and houses reappeared. After only a few moments, she was back on the sidewalk in front of 130 Middle Gate. She removed her phone from her pocket. The screen showed the date was Tuesday, September 24, 2024 and the time was 4 p.m. She was back on the same day and the same time as she had left.

CHAPTER 17

Tuesday, September 24, 2024

Margaret ran down the street to her house and through the front door. She dropped her backpack in the foyer and ran into the kitchen. Her parents were standing at the kitchen island.

"Hello," said her mom.

Margaret started to cry and ran toward her parents with open arms.

"What's wrong? Did something happen?" asked her mom, after Margaret stopped hugging them both.

Margaret took a deep breath and realized she would have to make up a story to tell her parents. "I'm fine. I had a tough day at school and was feeling quite down. I walked home, hoping to clear my head. I thought I was feeling better but when I saw you both in the kitchen I felt a real sense of relief. I think I was just a bit overwhelmed. I'll be OK."

"Are you sure? What happened at school? Do you want to tell us more about it? Would that help?" asked her dad.

"No, I'm good. I'll tell you all about it at dinner. I'm just glad to be home and I need to get upstairs and finish my history paper."

Margaret headed up to her room. She really was glad to be home but a part of her was sad and missed Charlotte.

Margaret finished researching Charlotte and Henry's lives. Charlotte did graduate with a Bachelor of Science degree in Pharmacy from the University of Manitoba and Henry did get a law degree from Osgoode Hall in Toronto. Charlotte and Henry were married in 1910. They moved into a new home, on West Gate, a year after they were married and lived in Winnipeg their entire lives. They had five children, three girls and two boys. Henry helped found the Law School at the University of Manitoba in 1914. After graduating, Charlotte worked for many years at McCullough Drug Store, the same drug store Margaret had seen in 1904 at the corner of Portage Avenue and Sherbrook Street. Charlotte did not stop working after she married nor after having children. She pushed the boundaries of what "polite society" expected of her. Not only did she work, but she was also involved in the community. She became a member of the board of the Winnipeg Children's Hospital in 1922, the Winnipeg Foundation in 1927, and the Winnipeg Ballet in 1941.

Charlotte and Henry were both committed to improving the lives of the people in Winnipeg's North End. They established numerous scholarships at schools, universities and colleges for those who lived in the North End. They also provided loans, grants and investments to individuals wanting to start their own businesses in the North End. Margaret found newspaper articles with photographs showing women and men receiving the grants and scholarships. One of the photographs identified Henry and Charlotte and indicated that it was taken at their home on West Gate, but it did not identify any of the other people in the picture. Margaret was sure she recognized Lucy and Jack in the photograph. She was glad to think of Jack starting his own business and Lucy becoming a teacher. She also found a picture of Henry and Charlotte taken with Billy when he was elected to city council, in 1920, representing the North End.

Charlotte and Henry were also both founding members of the Winnipeg Symphony Orchestra in 1948. Charlotte loved all types of music and even attended the first Winnipeg Folk Festival at Bird's Hill Park in 1974. When Margaret found a picture of Charlotte dancing at that Folk Fest, she pulled out her phone to find the picture she had taken of Charlotte dancing in Victoria Park. She smiled. Charlotte looked as carefree and beautiful in 1974 as she had in 1904. Charlotte died in 1975, at the age of 88. Henry had died three years earlier, at the age of 86. As Margaret wiped a tear from her cheek, she felt happy that her friends had led such wonderful and fulfilling lives.

It took almost two hours for Margaret to complete her history paper on Charlotte but when she was finished, she was excited to hand it in the next day. She was pleased with what she had written and so proud of Charlotte's many accomplishments. She was particularly happy that she had decided to include the pictures of Charlotte dancing at the Folk Fest and in Victoria Park. Her research had revealed one final aspect of Charlotte's life that Margaret wanted to check on right away. She went downstairs, found her mom in the kitchen and asked to borrow the car, explaining that she had almost finished her history paper but needed to check on one more thing.

When Margaret arrived at the St. James Cemetery, she thought to herself, "Was it only yesterday that I was here?" It took her a few minutes to find what she was looking for. There, in front of her, was a tombstone, not one she remembered seeing the day before, but one she had found while doing her research. It was engraved:

In Loving Memory of
Henry John Mills
1886-1972
Charlotte Claire Mills
1887-1975
Until We Meet Again

Margaret smiled at the epitaph, saying, "Rest in peace, my friends, until we meet again."

CHAPTER 18

Wednesday, October 2, 2024

Margaret had walked home from school and was in her bedroom re-reading her history paper, which Mrs. Sharpe had returned on Monday. Margaret had received an A+ and Mrs. Sharpe had written positive comments on her paper: "excellent research, well written and a pleasure to read." Her teacher had spoken to her at the end of the class, telling Margaret how much she had enjoyed the paper and, in particular, the photos.

"I loved the pictures, especially the one from 1904. You cited it as being from a Winnipeg heritage website, but the photo quality was so good, it looked like it was taken today, not over 100 years ago."

Margaret could not tell Mrs. Sharpe she had used her phone to take the photo. Instead, she replied, "I used some digital editing to enhance the quality of the original picture. I was pleasantly surprised by how well it turned out."

As she finished re-reading her paper, she felt a little strange. It had been only a week since the experience with Charlotte in 1904, but her memory of it was fading. Had it really happened? Had it been a dream? The pictures on her phone certainly helped make it seem real, but had she actually travelled through time? It did seem quite far-fetched.

The doorbell rang and Margaret went downstairs to answer it. When she opened the door there was a girl on the front step. She looked familiar but Margaret could not put a name to her face.

"Hi, Margaret. My name is Jenny Patterson. I go to BH too. I'm in grade 9," said the girl.

"Oh, yes, that's why you look familiar. Hi, Jenny. What can I do for you?" asked Margaret. She was curious as to why a grade 9 student would have looked up her home address and come to her house.

"Well, yesterday in social studies, Mrs. Sharpe gave us a copy of your history paper to read. She wanted us to see an example of a well written essay, which, by the way, it was and I enjoyed reading it," said Jenny.

"Thank you," replied Margaret, "you didn't need to come to my house to tell me that."

"That's not the real reason I'm here. I live over on West Gate. The house I live in has been in my family for many generations. My grandparents are David and Helen Mills, and the Charlotte Mills you wrote about was my great-great grandmother."

"Wow. That's crazy. What are the odds that I would write an essay about your great-great grandmother?" exclaimed Margaret.

"Well, that's not really the crazy part of this story. That starts after I showed my mom your essay. She read it and then she saw your name. You put your full name Margaret Jane Spears on it," said Jenny.

"Yes, I did. I don't normally put my middle name on essays but for some reason I did on this one," replied Margaret.

"Well, I don't even know how to describe the look on my mom's face when she saw your full name, but she was really excited and told me to follow her up to the attic. There was an old desk there and she opened one of its drawers and removed a metal box. Inside the box was a very old envelope. It was faded but still sealed. On the back of the envelope was written: 'From Charlotte Claire (Barbour) Mills' and on the front of the envelope was written..." Jenny reached inside her jacket pocket and handed something to Margaret. It was an old envelope addressed: "To Margaret Jane Spears, Armstrong Point, Winnipeg." Margaret stared at Jenny in shock.

"So, why is there an envelope from my great-great grandmother addressed to *you*?" asked Jenny.

"Well, Jenny, it's a small world, but that's Winnipeg. I think you need to come inside because this story is about to get even more crazy," smiled Margaret.

The End

ACKNOWLEDGMENTS

First, I must acknowledge the many online resources I used for historical information on Winnipeg. These included but were not limited to: the Manitoba Historical Society Archives, the University of Manitoba Digital Libraries Collection, Heritage Winnipeg, the National Centre for Truth and Reconciliation, Peel's Prairie Provinces-University of Alberta Libraries for *Henderson's Winnipeg City Directory* (1904) and the Internet Archive Digital Library for *Balmoral Hall 1901-2001: An Exceptional School Celebrates Its First Century* (2002). As well, I wish to acknowledge the books *Winnipeg 1912* by Jim Blanchard (2005), *The Foreigner* by Ralph Connor (1909), *The Time Machine* by H.G Wells (1895), *Looking Backward* and *Equality* by Edward Bellamy (1888, 1897) and *New Amazonia* by Elizabeth Corbett (1889).

Many thanks to Leslie Malkin, not only for being my editor but, more importantly, for being my friend since we were the two "new girls" in Grade 8, at Balmoral Hall.

I wish to say a huge thank you to Mom, Ryan, Sam, Peter, Catharine and Andrew for reading the drafts of my book and for making many inciteful suggestions and critiques, which improved it immensely. I am also extremely grateful to Ryan for helping me to designing the map of 1904 Winnipeg and for his fantastic catapult analogy.

Lastly, I must express my infinite gratitude to my

husband, Paul. He supported me as my idea for a story turned into written words on a page and finally ended in the completion of a book. Without his unwavering encouragement, my goal of becoming an author would not have been realized.

FOR THE READER

Thank you for reading *An Odyssey Home.* If you could leave a review on Amazon, it would be much appreciated. Reviews are incredibly helpful for authors.

I love to hear from readers. If you have any questions, comments or opinions to share with me, please emailed 1027Press@gmail.com.

BOOK 2 IN A TIME TRAVELLER'S ODYSSEYS

An Odyssey Abroad: An Irish Novella is available in paperback, as well as for kindle and in a large print edition.